DAVID SKIPPER was born in 1962 and grew
up on a housing estate in the heart of
industrial Teesside. An avid film fan, he
started at sixteen to write screenplays and
short stories and to make his own Super 8
movies. He is the author of two other novels
for young people, *Runners* (published by
Walker Books) and *Shadowshow*. He lives
in Cleveland, where, since leaving school,
he has worked as a laboratory technician.

Other books by David Skipper

Runners

QUEST

DAVID SKIPPER

To Annie,
Best Wishes
for Christmas

love
Dave .

WALKER BOOKS
LONDON

First published 1993 by Walker Books Ltd
87 Vauxhall Walk, London SE11 5HJ

Text © 1993 David Skipper
Cover illustration © 1993 Bruce Pennington

Printed and bound in England by Clays Ltd, St Ives plc

British Library Cataloguing in Publication Data
A catalogue record for this book
is available from the British Library.

ISBN 0-7445-2450-4

CONTENTS

1

THE WATCH

It was 3 a.m. and the town lay sleeping.

October wind rattled upstairs window-panes and rolled the grass outside in great black waves towards the sombre hills.

Three o'clock, murmured the old parish clock, hardly more than a dark speck far across the darker fields.

Three o'clock, rattled Tom Summerville's pocket watch.

Bats swooped.

Moths tapped.

Clocks ticked.

3.05, read the great iron hands on the old church steeple.

2.55, back-ticked the pocket watch above Tom Summerville's bed.

Backwards!

And that, in Tom's mind, was when it really

began – when the watch started backwards.

There had been other incidents before that; once his model jouster reared its colourful lance high into the air before grinding to a clockwork stop. Another time his scale model Chieftain tank motored across his bedroom floor without the aid of Tom or its own remote unit. But these things really only began after he got the pocket watch. Maybe it had some sort of magnetic power that affected toys. Or maybe there was another answer.

Next day, at school, Tom told Douglas.

"It's happening again."

Old Wilkins's back was turned. He was chalking a complex algebra problem on to the blackboard.

"What's happening again?" Douglas scratched his head with the end of his pencil.

"The haunting," Tom whispered and scanned the class to see if anyone had been listening. Everyone but Tom was copying from the board. Douglas too. Tom nudged him.

"Oh," his friend replied. And there the conversation ended, for Wilkins had turned. Pen in hand. Detention book ready.

After school, as the boys ambled along Grangefield Avenue, Tom glanced up from his tennis shoes, and there was the church that was engraved on the pocket watch, and suddenly he remembered.

"It's started again."

Douglas nodded. "You told me earlier."

"Don't you believe me?"

"I believe some dirty old pedlar fleeced you for a broken-down timepiece that sometimes overwinds and decides to go cuckoo."

"Oh, rubbish. Clocks don't go backwards when you overwind them. They don't go at all!"

They turned left into Maple Avenue. Tom walking backwards now, staring hard at the dark old spire that jutted up over the treetops like the world's first space experiment left to moulder and darken with the soot of a century's autumn bonfires.

"And it's not just the watch. Another of my light-bulbs exploded yesterday. That makes three, Doug. Three light-bulbs in a week. What do you say to that, Mr Professor?"

"I say your aunt Jess ought to get her house rewired."

They reached the bus-stop at 3.45.

At 3.50 they were travelling the narrow lane that led to home and the villages beyond. Tom looked out through the window to the spire above the trees. Douglas squinted down at the book in his lap:

$2x + 5y = 2 \quad 7x - 3y = 48$

SOLVE THE SIMULTANEOUS EQUATIONS.

WHATEVER METHOD IS USED, IT IS HELPFUL TO NUMBER...

"And my tank started up again!"

Douglas snapped the book shut, ran a hand through his neat chestnut hair and turned to his friend.

"Tom. You're *not* being haunted. You can't be. It's impossible."

"Nothing's impossible." They were his father's words, but on Tom's lips they lacked conviction.

"There are no such things as ghosts, Tom. No bogeyman. No tooth fairy. Nothing going to come out of your wardrobe at midnight moaning and groaning and rattling chains. And if you ever slip up and step on a crack in the pavement, you'll see that all that's going to happen is you'll squash a couple of bugs."

"Yeah," Tom murmured, thinking otherwise.

The rattly old minibus shuddered to a stop outside Tom's aunt's house, hissed open its doors and let the boys off.

Douglas turned to his friend.

Dark brown eyes to deep-water blue.

"No ghosts, Tom."

"Sure."

There the boys parted. Tom moved up the path of number nine Oakdene Avenue. Douglas moved up the path of number ten.

Both boys reached their homes in the same instant.

Douglas pushed on the doorknob and with

a cry of "Mum, I'm home!" let himself in.

Tom, with a similar yell of "Aunt Jess..." reached to do likewise, and suddenly it was summer again. Strangely the wind fell silent and the day became somehow warmer and brighter. And slowly, very slowly, after a quiet click of the door catch, the darkwood door, with its multicoloured window, swung quietly inward.

With a metallic cackle it stopped ajar.

Then simply, as simply as it had first seemed to change, the day returned to normal. Tom felt the autumn chill again.

Wind?

Yes. Tom shrugged as he stepped into the passage. Wind can blow a heavy door open.

But... Tom looked back at the door.

But wind can't click open a door catch, Tom. No matter how strong it's blowing. It's impossible.

Nothing's impossible.

"You're late!"

Startled, Tom caught movement in the polished brass doorknob and turned. Down the passage, between kitchen and dining-room, stood old Aunt Jess. Her plump hands holding out a steaming pie dish that smelt so warm and sweet and safe he was suddenly reminded of home. Of supper-times. Of Mum and Dad.

Quickly Tom blinked the memory away and shambled into the dining-room.

"Ah, Doug and me called in at the library to finish our projects."

"Douglas and I."

Tom sat. Jess sat.

"Projects, huh. About what?"

"Uh…" Tom shrugged. "You know, ghosts and stuff… Aunt Jess, do you believe in ghosts?"

Aunt Jess uncovered a dish, sending a salty cloud of steam swirling up to the ceiling. "Utter nonsense."

"Really?"

"Really."

"But … what about other things?"

"Other things?"

"I mean, well, what besides a ghost could make … ah, say, a vase fly across the room or … or a clock tick backwards?"

"Earthquakes and shoddy workmanship."

Tom looked up from his plate. Aunt Jess was smiling.

"Seriously."

"Seriously?" Jess tucked a straggle of hair behind her ear and frowned. "Well, I don't rightly know, Tom. There was a man on television once who claimed he could bend forks by simply looking their way. But I don't know if that was true or not. He never twisted any of my cutlery."

"Men that twist metal?"

For over a minute Tom stared at his fork,

but nothing happened except that his head got dizzy. He tested the fork with his fingers. It felt very solid.

Out in the hall, the clock chimed four.

Up in Tom's bedroom, his old Chieftain tank swung its great gun forward, travelled ten inches across the carpet, and then fell quiet again.

Tom finished his supper with impossible thoughts of ghosts and watches, shattering light-bulbs and men that twist metal keeping him silent.

The next night Douglas was in town with his parents and it was raining. Aunt Jess was downstairs watching an old love story on the TV, and Tom was in his room, searching the darkest corners for some way to pass the terrible, syrupy-slow time.

He had already drawn noughts and crosses until his head swam and counted the entire collection of green plastic soldiers he kept in a big cigar box above his wardrobe four times. (Still sixty-nine. One, a marine artilleryman, had gone missing at Christmas and had not been seen since.) The remaining soldiers he stood in battle formation along the far wall-skirting and, with the pistol that was once his father's, bombarded them with a hail of pellets. When even that had become boring, he had stared for a full five minutes at the fork he'd been carrying around ever since his conversation with Aunt Jess the day before.

But nothing happened.

Now, hunched at his bedside desk, Tom dusted down the barrel of the airgun for the thousandth time ...

and suddenly Tom was nine again. The carpet at his feet was grass. His chair, a blown-down oak tree. Wind blew warm and flapped something that was not the curtains. To his left, his mother: pretty face, pretty rose-patterned dress fluttering atop a red picnic rug. To his right, standing as tall and stately as the fallen oak must once have done: James Summerville. Tom's father, shooting at cans way across the field.

"Dad. That gun. It's not like others..."

Tom's father dropped beside him and handed him the gun.

"You like it?"

"It's beautiful," Tom said respectfully. "Will you, out of my savings, will you buy me one, someday?"

Dad laughed. Mum smiled.

Dad's arm dropped onto Tom's shoulder. "Sorry, Tom, but this gun is one of a kind. Can't be bought, sold, made or copied. But one day it may be yours. Someday I may tell you about it."

Tom handed the pistol back.

CRACK! Another can took flight...

14

* * *

Now Tom was older. Not his own age, but ten. The age he had been just before his parents were killed. He remembered now the day the old pedlar crossed his path. That strange old man whose appearance in town just happened to save his life.

It was a late summer afternoon. Tom recalled how the overgrown bridle-path leading to Rosethorn Cottage, his former home, had been so hazy with heatwave and ground mist that day that the tall grey man walking his horse and cart towards town seemed to appear out of nowhere. Tom remembered how this ragged, unshaved old man had asked directions to All Hallows Church, and before Tom could even pause for thought, away fluttered the canvas cover, out came the brass-studded chest and up flipped its lid.

"Young man, this just happens to be your lucky day. I have something here…"

Tom shuffled back, warily. His mother had warned him of men with such offers. The man was nothing but a gypsy seller.

"I have something here I'm sure you'll be interested in."

And Tom knew better, but what the heck, he couldn't resist. Cautiously he leaned over, peered in and saw the neat bundles of ivory tooth-combs, carved ash clothes-pegs, rainbow-coloured crocheted shawls and thick leather belts cut with strange pictures and an ancient language. And hidden among all of this – the pocket watch. It flashed golden light into Tom's eyes.

"That watch…"

"Ah," said the pedlar as if he had known all along. "The watch."

And within two minutes a deal had been struck.

Earlier that day Tom had bought Coke and chocolate and didn't have enough money left to pay for the watch outright. But the old man was staying in town a day or two, and if Tom agreed to help him polish his wares tomorrow, he could take the watch as payment. Tom had frowned. He had planned to spend the day boating on the lake with his parents … but it was such a beautiful watch – bright and finely scrolled like nothing he'd seen before. And the lake, well, that would be there next week, wouldn't it? So Tom agreed.

Next day, Tom kept his promise and spent the afternoon with the old man, who called himself Aaron. Polishing silver, waxing leather, carving wood. Talking and laughing, and even though he finished the day hot, tired and sweating, it hardly seemed like work at all. When he reached home he was told his parents were dead – a boating accident … explosion … nobody's fault.

Terrible … terrible.

That night the old gypsy left town. He was never seen or heard of in Greenvale again.

The memory burst like a pricked balloon and shocked Tom back to the present. And Tom, now thirteen again, pulled the watch from his wall. Dropping into the chair at his desk, pushing aside the books, the fork and the gun, he studied it closely. Its polished metal surface no longer shone the way it used to. Strangely, it looked older – much older in fact – and tarnished now. The etching of All Hallows Church on its back plate, once so faint he hadn't noticed it was there, was becoming engrained with a black gummy substance that made the picture clearer.

And backwards. It was still ticking backwards.

Shrugging, Tom hung the watch back over his bed, read a little, then polished his father's gun some more. Just when this was becoming a chore, his tank started up again.

With a familiar cry its gun turned foward. Tom glanced around. On the shelf above his desk, the tank's battery remote sat motionless. Next to it stood his torch and penknife, his coloured glass paperweight and his glow-in-the-dark, kit-built Frankenstein. But where was the Chieftain?

Tom scanned the room.

Nowhere!

Then movement caught his eye. By his bed, his library books sliding – volcanoes over dinosaurs over space stations and moon probes. The tank pushed them all aside. Across the floor it cut a path, straight and purposeful, as if on some secret mission that only it could accomplish. Tom's gaze followed the line. The tank was heading towards the soldiers grouped along the far skirting.

"Wow!" Gun in hand, now squatting stomach-down on the carpet, Tom followed the Chieftain like a wartime sniper through the sights of the pistol. His finger on the trigger. His father's voice in his head.

Don't pull the trigger, Tom. Squeeze it. Squeeze.

And the tank trucked on.

One foot from the skirting the first marine fell. Eight inches, another. Close to collison, the tank bagged five more.

Tom curled his finger, *squeezed* the trigger, smelt the smoke that spiralled skyward. And then, quite simply, as true as the moonlight that broke through Tom's window, as real as the wind that fluttered the curtains, the big old tank reached the thick wood skirting that lined the wall and with no loss of speed whatsoever, continued on through. Pushed past the wood and the paint and the bricks beneath it, as if it had encountered nothing stronger than a spider's web.

2

PASSING THROUGH

Gone.

Tom took the stairs four at a time ...

Vanished.

... startled Aunt Jess out of her fireside snooze, and blurting out all he could remember to include in the crazily disjointed manner of an over-excited six year old, rushed her up to his room. There he pointed, told, retold and swore as many oaths as he could think of to convince them both that it was true, all of it.

Aunt Jess had listened, frowned, followed, nodded, looked worried and checked Tom's brow with the palm of her big, warm hand. But she hadn't believed.

Up on the shelf sat the tank's remote unit. Back in the corner, next to the fallen books where it had first sprung to life, was the big old Chieftain itself.

Tom suddenly felt the supper in his stomach churn uncomfortably. "But..."

Aunt Jess knuckled the wall. It made a sickening sound of bone against brick. *Solid bone. Solid brick.*

"Solid, Tom, see? Must have dozed off. Dreamt it."

No, thought Tom.

"It's been a long day," Aunt Jess whispered as she brushed a curl of yellow hair from his eyes – the way his mother once did. "Tomorrow," she said, "you'll laugh."

But Tom hadn't heard. He was gazing out over the shadowy fields to the spire of the ancient All Hallows Church, thinking.

Not far away, at least in a sense related neither to time nor distance, a pedlar from an old town in an ancient county of a strange-named continent sat in the shade of a towering, soot-blackened oak tree. Watching. Listening. Quietly waiting.

But nobody came.

Next morning it was Douglas who took the stairs four at a time.

"What, Tom. What is it?"

Tom didn't answer. Without a word he took his friend's hand, and as if Douglas were the missing marine from his cigar box collection, arranged him into surveillance position against the far wall.

Douglas scanned the room, curiously. Nothing looked changed.

"Is it the fox cub, Tom. Did he come back?"

Tom couldn't restrain a chuckle. "No, Doug. It isn't the fox cub. Something better."

Lifting the tank's remote unit from his desk, Tom shuffled beside his puzzled-looking friend – close, so he could share in the gasp of amazement, feel his friend's startled shudder as if it were his own.

"Just watch and believe it."

With a pounding in his chest, Tom started the tank forward. Working it skilfully towards the red taped cross that now marked the point in the skirting where it had vanished yesterday.

"The tank." Douglas sighed. "I've seen this before."

Another urge to laugh, stifled.

"Not this, Doug. Believe me, not this."

Five feet away and the tank surged on, fresh batteries from the kitchen radio carrying it fast.

At four feet Douglas wiped sleep from his eyes and noticed, for the first time, the red cross taped onto the skirting.

Three feet. He turned to Tom.

Two. Tom looked at Douglas.

One. Both turned their attention back to the tank, and …

KER-RRACK! The scaled-down gun gouged a

21

canyon of paint and bounced back several inches.

Solid, Tom, see? Must have dozed off. Dreamt it.

The following silence was leaden. Douglas shuffled his feet and picked at a scab on his knuckle. Tom frowned so hard his eyebrows met and for one brief moment – just a second – wished that damned old tank had never driven through the wall at all. But of course it had. And nothing could ever change that. So …

"I … listen … I know this is gonna sound nuts, Doug, but last night … last night it drove right on through."

"Into the bathroom?"

"No. *Through the wall, Douglas. Through the wall. Vanished. And it turned up here.*" Tom gestured to the corner.

Douglas looked at his friend, close beside and yet a million miles away, and smiled wanly, pride tempered with concern.

Maybe these daydreams were Tom's way of handling the loss of his parents. Whatever the reason, they seemed important to him.

"So," Douglas said softly, "where did it go?"

Tom remained silent a moment longer, and then, without taking his eyes from the red taped X, whispered, "I don't know."

And quieter still. So quiet that Douglas didn't hear.

"But I'm going to find out."

Four days passed. Four long days of Geography and Maths and canteen lunches. Four long nights of staring at the wall and working the tank back and forth over the carpet until the batteries ran so low the steering failed, until the skirting was becoming battered, and the cracked old golf ball Tom had found while out in the park with Douglas last summer had been rolled at the cross so many times, usually tolerant Aunt Jess had eventually gone crazy about the noise it was making.

And nothing happened.

And eventually Tom had done what he had often considered doing, but for some strange reason he'd been wary of – he had tested the wall with his hands. Arms outstretched, fingers spread wide like wire antennae alert for danger signals, he had rested his palms on the smooth, blue-patterned surface and pushed, at first softly and then harder.

And nothing happened. Except…

Except the wall sent an electric charge of coldness into Tom's palms as he touched it. But that was fine because cold to Tom meant solid, immovable and above all, real. He allowed himself to breathe again.

With added confidence he leaned his weight on to his outstretched hands. And the wall remained – the wall. Strong and supportive.

Tom's solid-brick bedroom wall – not some paper-fine membrane just waiting to be broken.

Solid.

Tom kicked the skirting.

Solid.

He punched the plaster a little too hard and pain burned into his knuckles; but like testing a bruise or picking gently at a scabbed knee, it was a good hurt.

Solid.

Palms ahead of him, legs casual, he started forward.

And forward and forward and...

A purple darkness fluttered down like a shroud. The electrical hum that came with it caused Tom to think that another of his light-bulbs had blown. Then, seconds, long seconds later, he realized that the buzz did not stem from above and behind (the position of his overhead ceiling light) but from up ahead, tingling through his fingers like pins and needles.

Tom jerked his head back, startled. A blue electric spark jumped from his thumb to his forefinger. A short breath later another spark danced left thumb to right. Then suddenly, like November come early, sparks were everywhere – haloing Tom's hands into dark silhouette, sending a pulsing sensation along his arms so pleasantly strange that he forgot to be scared. For one moment he even felt the urge to laugh.

But Tom didn't laugh. For, like embers dying in a smoke-black fire grate, the blue sparks faded and a greater darkness fell. A dark so thick you could almost touch it.

Darkness.

Stillness.

Quiet.

And then, from nowhere you could point to – a distant sound, a strange sucking noise that exploded from faintest murmur to ear-splitting boom in little over a heartbeat.

There was light again. Neither too bright nor too dark. Soft, mellow daylight.

And in this daylight Tom saw fields and hills, distant trees and the more angular shapes of far-away buildings cut against a blue crystal sky that seemed to be lit from within, like a giant magic lantern scene.

And there, down beside his worn old tennis shoes, almost hidden among the coarse grass that grew in shadowy clumps along the field that sloped on down to a hedged lane, a hundred yards or so below – the marine – the old cigar box soldier that had gone missing all that time ago.

Tom bent close, studied the piece of plastic, but did not touch it. After a long pause he left it resting there in the grass and took a short step forward, tentatively testing the ground as if it were thin ice that might suddenly break with too much weight. But the grass yielded the way real grass should. Crunched underfoot and splashed up fallen rain, and beneath it the earth felt like ... earth. Firm. *Real*.

Tom took another step.

Another.

He could find his way back; the soldier marked the spot where he had ... "passed through" and up ahead – as a marker to the field itself – the tallest, most oddly twisted tree Tom had ever seen. You could probably spot it miles away, it was so tall and strange looking, and unlike the trees in the distance, this one stood alone and leafless, its bark burnt black as if it had been struck by lightning.

And of course he still had his gun. He had wedged it into the waist of his pants before stepping up to the wall. So here it was now, digging sharp into his back, hot and uncomfortable. But Tom was glad to feel it there.

On reaching the centre of the field Tom paused a moment to enjoy the pounding of his heart and sniff the warm, clover-scented air. Then slowly he started forward again, gazing over the patchwork ahead, noticing that, unlike the fields back home which had turned all sombre autumn browns, these not only held the summer colours of gold and brass and ripe-corn yellow, but some were speckled with reds and violets and deep-water blues, the same intense shade as the sky.

Without knowing it, Tom smiled. A wide, happy grin of a small child with a wonderful secret.

He moved faster across the field. Shoes slashing the grass the only sound. And the strange thing was, he didn't feel scared. There was something about this place that made Tom feel instantly at ease. Its warmth. Its stillness. Its quiet. Like a treasured moment held in memory, it seemed to radiate a feeling of tranquillity.

It was pleasantly warm though there was no sun. No wind.

There was light, but from no apparent source.

No sounds.

No movement.

And further down the field the thought suddenly came to Tom – it was as if he had somehow stepped into a beautiful landscape painting, and the only thing real in this magical world of paint and canvas was himself. Old Tom – flesh and blood – Summerville.

So he continued forward.

At the end of the field Tom unlatched a sun-bleached ranch gate almost overgrown by the thick hedging, stepped on to the lane and pulled it closed again. To his left the lane twisted down sharply and out of sight. To his right it rose smoothly up and round until a dense cluster of mature oak trees obscured its path further.

And to Tom's surprise, the surface of this lane looked like …

"Asphalt?"

He bent down to touch it. It felt like the surface of all the school playgrounds he had ever known: hot and coarse and yet somehow safe. Plain, old-fashioned, twentieth-century Tarmac.

Standing again, Tom glanced first left, then right.

And he suddenly thought of Douglas.

Early last year Tom had allowed himself to be talked into a series of Outward Bound lectures at the town hall. They were Douglas's idea but he managed only three. Old Colonel Friedman – scoutmaster general – treated a weekend amble into the woods like a month in the Amazon and did things with fresh killed rabbits that made Douglas violently sick. But the course did offer a few useful tips, like: *When in unfamiliar surroundings, height brings a better vantage point in which to survey your territory.*

Eyebrows knit to a thoughtful *V*, Tom started up hill.

He kicked at the ground.

Asphalt!

That was one of his theories exploded. This road surface belonged to the present – his present – not some Saxon, Norman or even prehistoric time period. And yet, his first impression, fired by the spectacle of that intense blue sky that reminded him of mediae-val stained glass window scenes, and those strange buildings in the distance, was that this place was not of the world Tom Summerville belonged to.

Thoughts began churning as he continued deeper into the lane. Distant memories of bed-time stories, gently whispered in his father's soft yet strong voice, tales of a magical land full of strange creatures and exotic places. Stronger memories of a Christmas play from long ago. Jack the Giantkiller. Thunder and lightning and a big, booming *Fee-fi-fo-fum* which scared him into tears.

And from two winters back, thoughts of a certain school day. Of sitting on the cool class-room floor in a great big circle. Douglas Clay-ton to his left, Billy Peterson to his right. And in the centre, book in her lap, Miss Fairfax.

And the story she read: of lions and witches and a mysterious wardrobe which, rather than ending in a hardboard back like most, ran on instead into a magical land of snow and ice.

But of course that was a story. Just a tale to tell kids at Christmas as a special treat to end the term.

But maybe the author kept a secret.

Maybe…

29

Tom stopped before he reached the brow and breathed long and deep.

Perhaps he was still in Greenvale. Maybe, in the next few seconds, he would step up to the brow and there, in the dip below, he would see the dark shadow of All Hallows Church, the glistening line of the brook, the hard edges of the town hall and the red market square, Greenvale from an angle never before viewed.

But there was doubt. Real doubt.

Was there any angle of town he and Douglas, over the last two years, had overlooked? Not likely. And if this place were Greenvale, then the town had suddenly frozen into an unnatural silence. The crows had finally stopped complaining. There was no murmur of distant cows. No cockerels, owls or blackbirds.

There was only shuffling footsteps, and they were his own.

One step. Two. Three. Four...

And down below, a fertile bowl opened up.

Golden fields.

Darker hedging.

Cumulus clusters of oak and elm.

And a silver snaking river which cut through a village that reminded Tom of drawings in a child's picture book. The houses seemed nothing more than stone boxes with two or three large windows and one great darkwood door, each topped with a too-big, off-centred chimney and thick yellow thatch.

Tom let his gaze drink further right, and there, like a dark reflection on the river itself, ran...

"A motorway. Without cars?"

Tom lowered himself onto a large clump of the springy grass and for a long while looked out over the land before him. Nothing stirred. Nobody moved either in or out of those strange looking novelty-cake buildings. No boats cruised the river. Not one car, cart, truck or cycle travelled the motorway.

But sometime later something did move down below – young Tom Summerville, travelling the deserted lanes while munching now and then from a handful of the biggest, sweetest blackberries he had ever pulled from a roadside hedge. Last one gone, he smacked his lips and wiped his mouth with the back of his hand.

It had probably smudged a great comet-tail of juice across his cheek, but what the heck. Who'd see?

Outside the first house, Tom stopped. It was bigger than it had seemed from the top of the hill but no less strange looking. Still oddly out of proportion and very basic. Its shuttered windows made Tom think of old crofters' cottages vaguely recalled from history lessons long ago. What were they? Seventeenth century? Eighteenth? Something like that. Douglas would know.

This particular house had its outside shutters closed but further along the narrow cobbled street there was a smaller house that appeared to have no window coverings at all. Simply three big squares cut out of the rough stone walls.

Taking a deep breath, Tom started for it, passing a grey stone wall and a cluster of red-berried shrubs to his right. While to his left he passed a group of those familiar oak trees, more of the fruiting bushes and a fast-food vending van.

Tom stopped.

A fast-food van?

He turned and peered through the leaves of the bushes growing between the trees, and…

Yes. Neither too old nor too new; here was a small fast-food van. The kind you see standing in parks selling ice-cream on hot days, or burgers and hot soup in the winter months. It was painted red and white and was trimmed with well-polished chrome.

For closer inspection Tom pushed his way into the shrubs. They had no thorns and yielded easily. The tyres bore the faded marking: SP 7OO DUNLOP EXTRA-GLIDE.

Dunlop!

Nothing seventeenth century about them.

Cogs began turning in Tom's head. A thousand questions set in motion in an instant. But as soon as they had come, all were gone as puzzlement and wonder were replaced by a fear that shook his entire body.

For something touched him.

Something had laid a hand on his shoulder. A great, cold, and terribly old hand.

Tom froze as terror made his flesh crawl. For a moment his head felt dangerously light. But because fear of facing whatever was breathing down his neck was slightly less than the absolute terror of passing out cold in the dark shadows of this place, he fought to keep from fainting and slowly turned.

And what he saw was this: a two-years'-gone memory of a man he met on a Greenvale bridle-path during one certain hot summer's day.

Like the trees, he was tall. A tall thin man dressed in the faded rags of an old gypsy; a once green, now brown tunic and moth-eaten grey pants, and a long baggy overcoat so old that all colour had long since died from it. Beneath the shadow of a brown felt hat Tom noticed that his face was as pale as the clothes he wore. But his eyes still had life. They were as blue as the sky. Young eyes in an old face.

It was the face of the pedlar man.

The old man reached for Tom.

Tom stepped back.

"The watch, Tom," said the pedlar eagerly. "Have you brought it with you?"

Tom shook his head slowly. "I don't understand."

"Come," said the pedlar. "I must tell you."

Five minutes later, Tom found himself sitting in the house he had been heading towards before he had stopped to look at the van.

It was a small, one roomed building, dimly lit by what light found its way in through two squares cut into the dark, grey stone walls. The floor was unevenly paved, with just one (but one extremely large) animal pelt rug spread before a burning hearth. The only furniture was two wooden high-backed chairs and a small roughly made table. To Tom it looked like cheap garden furniture that had been left out in the rain too long. The chairs were very hard, school canteen uncomfortable. On the table was a large, green glass bottle and two grey metal goblets. The pedlar filled the goblets with liquid from the bottle, kept one and handed the other to Tom.

"My name is Aaron," said the old man. "Do you remember me?"

"Yes," said Tom, taking the goblet and sniffing its contents cautiously. It smelt flowery, like violets. "You're the man I met on the bridle-path going into town."

"Yes."

"Do you live here?" Tom asked as he gazed

through the window to the yellow fields in the distance.

Aaron shook his head. "Only when passing from your land to my own."

"Where are we?"

"This is the Farposts."

Tom frowned. The name sounded strange to him, but he had been expecting stranger. Something like Middle Earth or Never Never Land. He took a sip of the liquid Aaron had poured him and was pleased to find it tasted as sweet as it smelt.

"You were not told of this place? This or the next?"

"The next?" Tom sat up. "Told what? No. All I know is that ever since that stupid watch of mine started ticking backwards, life's been like one long day-dream."

Tom looked up from his goblet. The old man was staring at him. Not just looking, Tom noticed uncomfortably, but scrutinizing him as if he were a museum exhibit. Tom cleared his throat.

"You said something about my watch."

Aaron put down his goblet and sat up. His face had become suddenly grave.

"We need the watch, Tom. You have to return it."

"But it's mine. You gave it to me."

"I entrusted it to you, for safety. Now it needs to be returned."

Tom reached for his wrist. "If it's that important you can have mine. It's OK really. I know it looks good, but from where I come they're really quite cheap. Quartz, see?" He pointed at the numbers, not realizing they had stopped shifting the moment he had passed through. "These things are incredibly accurate, and they never run backward—"

Two large hands folded over Tom's own.

"You don't understand, Tom. We need the pocket watch I gave you. No other. You must return it."

Tom felt his chest tighten, for the light had suddenly gone from the pedlar's eyes, and his sweet low drawl had taken on a shaky, desperate edge.

"You must take it to the Dark Tower and free Prince Tyso."

"The Dark Tower?" was all Tom could manage to say, but he noticed with these few words that his own voice had become high and startled.

"Yes. The Tower beyond the Pitch Forests. It will be a dangerous task, but until Prince Tyso is free and the false Prince Aldred destroyed, our land can never be at peace..."

The old man continued speaking but most of the words faded from Tom's mind. The few that broke through made little sense.

Pitch Forests. Barricades. Evil Princes.

The story Aaron was telling was beginning

to sound like a crazy game of Dungeons and Dragons: *Do not pass go. Do not collect two hundred rubles, and do not, whatever you do, get involved in any screwball scheme to over-throw the evil prince and restore peace to a land which seems just fine the way it is.*

Tom stood, and calmly, like an actor playing a role, he turned to Aaron and said, "I have to go now."

"We need your help, Tom."

Tom started for the doorway. Aaron stood but made no attempt to stop him, although his eyes, Tom noticed, emphasized the words he had spoken. WE NEED YOUR HELP!

"Be careful, Tom. Your power is growing. It shines like the Golden Star. Now that our worlds are again at their closest, if you do not use it to destroy Aldred, he will use it to find you and…"

But Tom, moving faster now, had gone.

3

ALDRED

Back in the autumn country of Greenvale, life continued turning. A thousand watches surged three days forward. One turned another three days back. The nights were drawing in darker and the town park was empty, save for two dark shadows braving the wind: Tom Summerville and Douglas Clayton, sitting, but not swinging, on the deserted leaf-blown swings.

Tom was unusually quiet.

Douglas was quietly thoughtful.

For a long time the night remained silent, then:

"Tom, what's wrong?"

"Uhm ... what?"

"What?" Douglas sat up so sharply the chains clanked.

"For the past three days, Tom, you've been wandering round town like you've got toothache during exam week."

Tom remained silent. Douglas bit his lip; it was two years to the month since Tom's parents had been killed. Sometimes Douglas lay in bed wondering how that must feel.

"October blues, uh?" Douglas said gently.

"Just a little bored." Tom shrugged away the truth easily. How could he tell Douglas what he was thinking. How could he expect Douglas to believe when he could hardly believe it himself?

He dropped his gaze back to the shadows at his feet and quietly sighed.

Somewhere deeper in the park a much darker shadow moved. Sniffing the air like a hound on scent.

Searching.

Getting close.

Closer...

"Bored, uh?" said Douglas, kicking out at a pebble that lay almost in his path.

The boys had given the park up for some warmer time when the wind wasn't blowing so strongly and the clouds didn't threaten to spoil the night with rain.

"Well, let's see. We've been swimming and conkering. Played battleships and hangman. Visited old man Marchant and raided the orchard next door. And still you're bored?"

Tom barely heard the question, but nodded

anyway. Doug's tone seemed to require it.

"Oh, I know. We could go to the church."

"The church?" Tom stopped. Somehow it seemed important.

"Yeah," said Douglas. "All Hallows. They're pulling it down because someone important said it was unsafe. Bad foundations or something. There's trucks and tractors everywhere."

"Oh," said Tom. Oh, he thought. Tractors, how dull. His shoulders dropped and he shambled on again, thinking. And again Douglas chewed his lip. Douglas Clayton frowned hard – worried.

"Tom…"

"Doug. You know how we sometimes light a candle in your room, and when its dark read a story from those old magazines we found?"

They were Hotspur paperbacks full of picture stories of commando raids and jungle adventures.

"Uhm," mumbled Douglas curiously. His friend was looking ahead now as if he were seeing something out there in the darkness that Douglas could not. "Yes. I know."

"And how," Tom went on, "how we always said that even though dangerous things happen and sometimes people got killed, we'd still do it if we had to. Well … would you? Really?"

Douglas paused. Tom had turned. He was

looking Douglas straight in the eye now. "I ... well, I guess if I thought I could make a difference. If somebody really needed my help then I suppose—"

"You could be killed. Killed or abandoned alone somewhere miles from home."

Douglas looked at Tom thoughtfully. From the way Tom had spoken, it sounded as if he considered being abandoned and alone far worse than being killed. Finally Douglas said, "Yes."

"You'd do it?"

Douglas nodded. It was the answer Tom seemed to want.

"But why ask, Tom? Things like that just don't happen in real life. At least not any place near here."

"Oh, you'd be surprised, Doug."

Tomorrow, thought Tom. Tomorrow morning I'll do it.

Tom dropped a hand on his friend's shoulder and spurred them both on, until Douglas stopped abruptly.

"Tom, you've been acting really strange lately. Is there something wrong?"

And standing there in the murmurings of a town winding down for the night, all Tom could do was laugh.

On again, and the hedged lane leading towards home was at its darkest now. Stirring alive with the evening sounds of wind whispering through the autumn hedge and the occasional night creature panicking among the fallen litter. Now and then bony fingers of hawthorn branches brushed against their legs – but no more than usual. An invisible spider's line broke across Tom's face. Then something happened.

Douglas pulled him to a sudden stop. For there, far down the lane, standing dark against the light of a street lamp far away and behind, was the shape of a man. It was tall and unmoving, blocking the centre of the lane like a black iron traffic bolster defying anything to pass it. Although no light fell on it, Tom knew that it was facing forward; and not *just* facing forward, but facing *him*. Watching ... studying.

And it was Aldred. Aldred, the evil prince Aaron had spoken of. Tom knew this with complete certainty – as if they had met before and all this had already happened, as if it were a recent memory being vividly recalled.

Here's the part where he ... what?

Here's the part where he raises his hand, points his finger and I, for no reason I can think of, push both Doug and me to one side.

The hedge to their right, the place where they had stopped before Tom darted them away, puffed into a ball of brilliant white fire. From their crouched position in the hedge opposite, Tom and Douglas prickled with the heat from it.

Scorching smells turned the air sickly.

The Aldred shape glided one step forward.

Tom sprang to his feet, pulled his dazed friend up and taking his hand like a harried mother with a stubborn child, hurried him back in the direction they had come. Into the darkness. Into the night.

"Come on, Doug, quickly."

"But, Tom—"

"Hurry!"

Another ball of fire, crackling, painting trembling shadows, exploded somewhere behind.

Tom didn't look back. Birds flew up, screeching, flapping wildly. Out ran creatures usually too shy, too timid to announce their existence. And following, almost as fast, two bigger but equally startled creatures – Tom and Douglas.

A million times they had travelled the lane. Counted it step for step. Tonight it seemed far longer than ever before.

More steps. Douglas slowing. Tom, pulling twice the weight, weakening. Tom could hear Douglas panting like a terrified animal, but of himself all he could hear was his heart pounding like thunder.

Another ball of fire rose up, but this was further behind. The heat from it wasn't so intense.

The burning smell was milder, easier to stomach.

Tom stopped. Douglas almost ran into him. Way down in the hedge there was a narrow gap. A very narrow gap indeed.

Sometimes you see a small animal squeeze its plump body through a hole no bigger than a pencil shaft, as if the creature had bones of rubber that must fold in and stretch longways to allow this to happen. Now Tom was that creature. Squeezing, writhing, ignoring the burning cuts the sharp thorns caused. And all the time never leaving hold of Douglas's hand.

Through.

Douglas next. Slightly smaller, scrambling, clawing with growing panic – like a poor swimmer diving into deep water and not surfacing fast enough.

Finally through.

And together across the field. Fast. Towards the orange lights of the road beyond it...

Over the creek. Across the churchyard, too hurried to be scared. Through the lych-gate, over the stile...

Towards home.

Not looking back.

Not daring to.

Tom's room. Ten minutes later.

Douglas, still breathing hard, lay on top of the bed gazing way beyond the ceiling, his brow wrinkled in confusion. Tom, his straw-coloured hair turned darker with sweat, paced from window to door to desk and back again. His father's gun tight in his fingers. His heart still pounding like a kettledrum at his temples. Neither had spoken since gasping a fast, falsely innocent "See-ya" to Aunt Jess as she left for her weekly game of bridge at the Thorntons' house on their return.

Then finally Douglas rolled onto his side and looked at Tom, who had settled at his desk – not sitting, but leaning alert against it. Douglas's words came slowly and evenly. Spoken with the care and effort of a person trying hard not to cry.

"Tom ... what was that thing?"

Aldred! Tom thought coldly. That, believe it or not, Douglas, was the Prince of Darkness.

Tom shrugged. "I don't know, Doug. Maybe it was ... well, you know how in the dark everything looks different and you sometimes think you see things that aren't really there ... well—"

"It tried to *kill* us, Tom."

Douglas didn't sound frightened. He sounded terribly upset. "He wanted to kill us! What kind of people do things like that?"

Tom wished he could say something clever. Something light that would brighten the situation and make it seem as if nothing bad had happened. Instead he looked at Douglas and shook his head.

"There're a lot of crazy people about, Doug. A lot of bad things happen. You just never think they're ever going to—"

Tom broke off. In an instant Douglas had sprung to his feet, scrambling to the window, his eyes big and round.

"What if it followed us, Tom? What if it comes after us?"

Tom shook his head, but pulled a pellet from his drawer and loaded the gun anyway.

"He can't have followed us, Doug. He'd never have got through the hedge. And even if he had, he couldn't have kept pace. I bet we set a new land-speed record tonight. And anyway, Doug, chances are we're both—"

Tom stopped. Downstairs, something rattled.

But it was only Aunt Jess. Of course, it had to be. Aunt Jess, probably forgotten something and come back quick.

Except it wasn't.

Tom almost screamed. Douglas was suddenly behind him. Clutching the material of his jacket and breathing hot panicky breath down his neck.

"Listen, Doug." Tom broke free and turned. "Don't get crazy. It's probably just—"

Down below something cracked. Not far away, a door crashed inward.

Footfalls now, climbing. Slow. Heavy. *One. Two. Three...* Tom looked to the window. Aunt

Jess's house was old and tall. It was a long drop on to hard stone...

Four. Five. Six...

to his bed. A barricade? No. Above it.

The watch. Its fine antique chain snapped easily as Tom yanked it down.

Seven. Eight. Nine...

"Doug?" he said. But Douglas was staring at the door – the white painted door that ran into the landing at the top of the thirteenth stair – like a terrified creature staring into the blinding light of a fast approaching vehicle.

Ten. Eleven. Twelve...

Quickly, Tom wedged the gun into the waist of his jeans,

Thirteen...

took Douglas's hand in his own and pulled him towards the wall.

Towards it.

And through it.

The first time Tom had "passed through" it had happened slowly. This time it was faster. Perhaps because on this occasion he had thrown caution to the wind and raced on through. Everything that happened before – the dark, the tingling and sparks, the explosion of sound and blackness to light and the quick fading haze – did so again.

But this time it all happened in an instant.

After squeezing his right hand to make sure

Douglas had crossed over too, Tom opened his eyes. At his feet was the old cigar-box soldier. His marker. He had entered at the exact point he had entered and returned the first time. Here was the soldier. There was the grass. And ahead towered the old soot-blackened oak tree. Blackened perhaps by the same force Aldred had used in the dark, deserted lane less than …

less than an hour ago.

Could Aldred follow them through? Or did everybody have their own special passing point?

Tom looked at Douglas with concern. His eyes were wide and his mouth had fallen into an astonished O. He didn't speak and gave no resistance when Tom pulled him forward.

"Come on, Doug. We have to get away from here. I'll try and explain as we go on, OK? Right, Douglas?"

But if Douglas replied at all, it was so quietly that Tom did not hear.

4

THE KEY

Nothing had changed.

The warmth. The light. The summer yellow of the fields and that strange silence.

Tom led Douglas across the field, through the gateway at the end of it, and up the asphalt lane that ran towards the dip where the houses nestled. By this time Douglas was keeping pace, so Tom released his hand.

"Doug ... I know I said I'd explain everything to you, but ... but the fact is, I don't know much more about this place than you do. I'm going to see somebody who might be able to tell us more."

Tom wasn't sure if Douglas had heard. Nothing registered on his face and he did not ask questions the way Douglas usually did. But Tom continued anyway. "He's an old man called Aaron. The pedlar I met on the lane two years ago, remember? He's a little strange but he is a friend, so there's no need to be scared. OK?"

Douglas remained silent, but the dazed look, Tom noticed, seemed to have faded from his eyes a little. Now Douglas, instead of staring forward like a zombie as he had to begin with, was looking everywhere. Staring up at the towering trees, far across the purple and red speckled fields, to the hills way off. Scanning the deep blue sky for sun or moon, birds or vapour trails. The way Tom himself had done.

"You see, Doug, there's something I've got to do. I'm not really sure what exactly. But I think it's important."

The old man was sitting up against the outside wall of his house, puffing on a long clay pipe as he watched the boys approach.

Some distance away, Tom nudged Douglas. "That's the man I was telling you about. I think he knows what's going on."

For almost a minute Douglas remained silent. Then, as they got closer and could see a little better, he squinted and said dreamily, "He looks like Huckleberry Finn, Tom."

And Tom, noticing the hat and the pipe, the ragged clothes and the carefree slouch of the old man's shoulders, agreed.

The world's oldest Huckleberry Finn.

* * *

"The watch," Aaron said, even before the boys had reached him. "Did you bring the watch?"

"Yes," Tom replied. He stopped before Aaron and quickly reached into his inside pocket. He had zipped it in there for safety, and ... he reached down further – strange – he couldn't feel the smooth, round piece of metal anywhere. Don't say he'd lost it. It was such a wonderful watch. He tried his other pockets, perhaps in the confusion he had slipped it in the back of his jeans instead. But no, it was not there. It must be in his jacket pocket. He tried again. If he had lost it, how would he...

But wait, there was something there after all. It didn't take Tom long to realize that it wasn't the watch. Even without seeing it, he could feel that it was the wrong shape entirely. It was bigger than the watch, and as he caught it in his fingers he realized that it was much heavier too.

The object Tom pulled into the daylight was a rusty iron door key. It was not Tom's key or any of Aunt Jess's. In fact, it was at least five times as big as any key Tom had ever seen before. Tom stared at it in surprise.

"I don't understand. I had the watch with me. I zipped it in my pocket, I'm sure of it."

Aaron plucked the key from Tom's fingers and studied it keenly. "In your world it became the watch so that *he* could not find it. Now that you are of an age to use it, it has become its true self again."

"You mean," Tom began, feeling a little stupid and not at all sure if he hadn't missed something important, "this is the watch that hung over my bed?"

Aaron nodded.

"But how?" This was Douglas's first real question since they had walked through the wall.

"An ancient power that some call Enchantment."

Aaron motioned the boys to sit, then after rummaging in the grey cloth sack leaning up against the wall beside him, he brought out a roll of something which was neither cloth nor paper but a mixture of both. It looked like a rotting old comic, rolled up and tied in the middle with a thin blue ribbon.

Aaron offered the roll to Tom. It was stained with yellow patches and both ends were ragged. It felt damp and smelt musty. Tom looked at it uncertainly.

"Open it," said Aaron.

Tom glanced at Douglas and his friend nodded encouragement. The ribbon was so worn that it broke the moment Tom pulled at it. The disagreeable smell became stronger as the roll flopped open. Tom noticed that there was writing on the material although at first he could barely make it out, it was so faint and

odd-looking – fancy, old-fashioned writing.
Some of the letters were facing the wrong way.
Douglas leaned closer.

"What does it say?"

Holding the roll close to his face, Tom
squinted hard.

"'The Scroll of the Seventh Season,'" he
began, then immediately stopped because the
first few lines had faded to a blur. He began
again when he found the first line he could
understand.

> *Now our King's power and all it gave*
> *Is stole away, our prince enslaved*
> *Within a tower, tall and bare*
> *And only one can enter there.*

Below this was another piece too worn to be
read. Tom broke off and looked at Douglas,
who urged him to go on. Tom cleared his
throat, then continued reading a little way
further.

> *Go through a tunnel deep and grave*
> *Its dark demands you to be brave*
> *Then over fields that once raised seed*
> *To where the trees and giants feed*
> *Next cross the flat and hueless land*
> *And watch for dangers in the sand*
> *Then travel fast and travel light*
> *On to the place where day meets night*

Where it lies no one can say
An arch, perhaps, will show the way
Climb the steps as fast as you can
But beware the evil –

Douglas yanked the Scroll his way. "Beware the evil what?"

Tom shrugged. The bottom corner of the Scroll had been torn away. Douglas looked at Aaron, who was filling his pipe with powder from a small leather pouch. The old man looked up and simply whispered, "In Edonia these days you must be wary of everything. What is written on the Scroll is true, Tom. The true heir to our land is locked away. Until he is set free Edonia will continue to suffer the wickedness of his false cousin Aldred."

A thick silence descended like a cloud. It was Douglas who finally broke it. "Why is the prince locked away?"

"Because of the Old Power." Aaron drew on his pipe but did not light it. Douglas wondered how he would light it if he wanted to smoke. "Ever since history was first written," said Aaron, "the rulers of our land have possessed a great power. A magic that could make a sword rise high into the air simply by wishing it. The Power could whip the wind into a whirling storm or calm a raging stream. Those with the Old Magic could pass into other worlds, including yours."

Could they, Tom wondered, bend a fork by merely looking its way? Or ... *or cause a bush to burst into flames by simply pointing a finger at it!*

"Is Aldred one of them? Is Aldred a ruler?"

"The Great Rulers no longer exist. Aldred and our prince, Tyso, are descendants of the Rulers from long ago. One from our world, one from yours."

"From our world?" said Tom.

"During the time your land was in the shadow of its own troubled dark age, ours was ruled by King Titan, a good man who brought peace and prosperity to all Edonians. He was a wise and virtuous leader, but he was a dreamer. His weakness was beauty, not battle."

Douglas tutted. Tom shushed him.

"One day, when travelling to Outlands – your land – the king met a beautiful gypsy dancer. The moment his gaze fell upon her his heart was lost—"

"So he brought her here," suggested Tom. This was how all those tales seemed to go: The noble king carries the beautiful maiden back to his land on a fine white stallion and—

Aaron shook his head. "Here the girl was forbidden. The king returned and tried to forget her, but his heart was broken. After many nights of unhappiness he gave up his crown and chose to spend the rest of his days in your land as an ordinary citizen. His brother, Prince Olav, took to the throne and by all accounts ruled Edonia well."

"What has this to do with the man on the lane ... Aldred?"

"The king who returned to your land wed the gypsy girl, had children."

"Descendants," said Douglas.

Aaron nodded. "Descendants possessed powers similar to the king's. But not as strong. Not as controllable."

"And Aldred and Tyso," asked Tom, "are descendants of those children?"

"Tyso is a descendant of the prince who stayed. Aldred is a descendant of the king who left."

Douglas wondered if there were others.

"There was a time when there were many. But with the passing of the seasons their numbers have grown fewer. Unable to handle their power, some were destroyed by it. Others were killed out of jealousy or fear. Many simply lost their power and became ordinary citizens, like the old king. And now," the old man sighed, "since James Summerville was killed two harvests back, the line is almost at an end."

James Summerville.

Immediately Tom heard that name, his father's name, he jolted forward and looked more closely at Aaron, expecting to find the words entering his head not quite matching the movement of Aaron's lips. But they did match and Aaron continued talking about Tom's father and the old king as if nothing were wrong.

Douglas flashed Tom an expression of astonishment, then looked at Aaron. "Tom's father was a descendant?" he said breathlessly.

"A distant descendant of the abdicated king. And of course Tom is too. That is why we need him. Only a Descendant can enter the Dark Tower."

Aaron put down his pipe and looked at Douglas. Beside him, Tom's face had taken on the same vacant expression that Doug's had on first entering the Farposts.

"Until recently our land was ruled by Prince Tyso's father. He governed, like his ancestor Titan, with wisdom and grace rather than the magic and mayhem of the Dark Ages. Aldred came from the Outlands, passing himself as the prince's cousin whom he had murdered, and disagreed with these policies. Aldred had the king executed as a traitor to the old ways and his son banished to the Tower beyond the forests."

Aaron placed the key before the boys. "This is the key to the cell in which Aldred keeps the rightful heir to our land imprisoned."

Douglas studied Tom. He had silently picked up the key and was now examining it closely.

"And you want Tom and me to go there? Go there and free the prince?"

"You may travel with Tom, but only a Descendant can enter the Dark Tower in which the prince is locked without falling foul of its evil enchantment."

A worried look fell across Doug's face, drawing his dark eyebrows closer. "Will it be dangerous? I mean, even for a Descendant?"

"Descendants are not invulnerable. Tom's father was a wise and courageous man and in his visits to our land he did good and noble things. Yet he is now dead."

In a throaty whisper, Tom asked if his father came here often.

"When he was able," answered Aaron. "When our world and yours passed close to each other and the Power of the Old Kings was at its strongest."

Tom looked down at the key again. "How did you get this from Aldred? If it was important to keep the prince imprisoned, wouldn't he have put it somewhere safe?"

"Aldred believed that he had. Fearing that someone loyal to the Old King might steal the key from him, he rode out to the Crystal Lake of Olam. He strapped the key to an arrow and fired it far out into its deadly waters. There, at the bottom of the lake among the blind, flesh-eating creatures that inhabited its depths, he assumed it would stay. And probably it would have were it not for his own terrible ways." Aaron paused and drew on his pipe. "But the lake dried up. An old fur trapper saw the arrow protruding from the bed among the bones of the flesh-eaters and found the key, still bound to its shaft. That was several harvests back. The last time our worlds passed close, the Old Power was not strong enough for us to call you."

"Is it now?" asked Tom.

Aaron did not reply. Tom's eyes pressed him for an answer.

"Only you can answer that, Tom," said Aaron as he picked up the sack and creaked slowly to his feet. He heaved the sack over his shoulder. It made a strange clanking, rattling, knocking sound as if filled with a little bit of everything.

"Come now, we've wasted enough time. If Aldred has news of our plans he will try and stop you. I can take you as far as the Subway, but I can not be seen with you in Edonia. From the Subway you must go on alone."

There was no sign of darkness falling. Tom was beginning to doubt that there ever would be. They had been travelling for over four hours, Aaron leading, often straying from the asphalt lane in favour of short cuts over fields of sweet-smelling clover and heather, and occasionally wheat so tall it buried the boys completely.

Tom savoured the experience. That last time he and Douglas tried it back home in the familiar variety they were quickly run off the land by an angry red-faced farmer.

The strange grey buildings that Tom had first seen only as faint outlines on the horizon were closer now. Tom could make out their shape. They were castles. Great triangular masses of towers and turrets that rose up out of the golden fields like the tubes of some magnificent pipe organ. They were very puzzling. Here were ancient – though perfectly preserved – castles. Further away there was something which looked like a giant television mast. Earlier they passed a huge electric pylon, and now, marking the brow of another hill was a –

Tom swallowed, Douglas stopped and blinked.

– a hangman's gallows.

A rotten, ancient gallows so tall and dark it swept away all the aches and the tiredness the fifteen miles of ups and downs had begun to cause. To Tom, although the rope hung thankfully empty, it was a reminder of the dangers that might lurk behind the blinding wonders of this place. He glanced to Douglas beside him. He was gawping at the gallows, but no more than he had at the castles.

Another hour passed. Another four miles.

Tom's legs were aching and he could feel

blisters forming on the soles of his feet.

Still no sign of darkness falling.

And finally, in the shade of a cluster of elm trees growing beside a vast lake that reflected the blue of the sky exactly, they stopped. Douglas tugged off his neat-pressed jacket and, after scrunching it into a pillow, dropped it and himself at the base of one of the trees. Within seconds he was asleep.

Nothing else stirred.

As Aaron moved on up the lakeside bank to view the surroundings, Tom looked down at Douglas and thought back to the gallows. He was glad that Douglas was with him in this strange land, but it was a feeling tempered with concern for his friend's safety. If anything happened to Douglas it would be his fault.

It was his watch that started it. His *watch*. His *tank*. His *wall*. Whatever had to be done, had to be done by himself alone.

He would, he decided right there and then, leave Douglas in Aaron's charge until the task was done.

Tom leant back against the tree-trunk and although the temperature had dropped not a single degree, he zipped his jacket further.

Some time later, something moved.

But it was only Douglas, stirring in his sleep. For a long while Tom sat against the tree listening to the comforting sound of his soft breathing. When Aaron returned, Tom, his head slumped against Douglas's shoulder, was sleeping too.

And still no sign of darkness falling.

5

THROUGH A TUNNEL, DEEP AND GRAVE...

In Edonia the next day, within the walls of Castle Crestoban, Aldred was sitting in conference with his senior Knight of the New Order and a mystic from the Shadow Hills. The old fortune-teller was telling of a boy and a key and a battle to come.

Far away, in Tom Summerville's home town of Greenvale, it was still dark. Still night. Since the boys passed through, a scant twenty seconds had passed.

Out in the Farposts, time had surged forward. But not so much as a leaf changed. It was peaceful, for a time.

Then Tom woke with a start – for Douglas, beside him, screamed himself out of a terrible dream. Now bleary-eyed, he gave the area the briefest of scans, then looked at Tom and said, "It is real, isn't it?"

"Yes," Tom answered and glanced around. Aaron was still there, but now he was sitting further along the lakeside, gazing out over the water, puffing again on that long clay pipe of his. Tom could see the thick white smoke rising up to the sky in a thick vertical line.

Douglas leaned back against the tree and looked out over the lake. "You know, Tom, I thought it was a dream. At first I did."

"Maybe it is," suggested Tom, not believing it for a moment.

Douglas shook his head. "No, I don't think so. Everything's too real. Dreams aren't like this."

For a long time they sat gazing out over the water in silence, then finally Douglas rubbed his chin, let out a sigh that wasn't entirely hopeless and turned to Tom. "Are you really going to do it?"

"I don't think I have much choice, Doug. I know it sounds bad, but I have a feeling something worse will happen if I don't free Prince..."

"Tyso."

"Yes. Prince Tyso. A real prince, Douglas. Can you believe it?"

Douglas looked at Tom with surprise. "Tom, last night we were attacked by some guy with flame-thrower fingers, then a couple of minutes later we walked straight through your bedroom wall. Heck, right now I think

I'd believe just about anything..."

The guy with flame-thrower fingers.

Suddenly Tom felt his throat tighten as he thought back to, not a dream, but a distant memory.

The road outside Tom's house was quiet as usual and Tom was small. Just a little boy who kicked his big old football high over the garden fence, and there in the centre of the quiet road it came to a sudden rest, as if a magnet had somehow held it there. It never rolled to the side the way it usually did...

Of course, Tom had been told never to step onto the road even if it was very quiet with little traffic. But when you are five years old you are told you *should not* so many times that the *should nots* sometimes got a little confused with the *must nevers* and...

Tom reached up and unlocked the gate. Looked left. Looked right. Looked forward.

There was the ball, in this quiet lane only six short steps away.

Now five. Now four. Three...

Now here it came. The car. The big, fast, roaring lion of a sports car which pounced round the hawthorn bend at unbelievable speed. Fast and faster. Its snarling chrome grille sucking up the road on which young Tom Summerville stood frozen in terror.

Fast, faster...

Close, closer, closer...

And in this instant in which even a little boy could realize the depth of his mistake, he saw the man behind the wheel. A man with the rusty colour of hate in his eyes and wiry coils of raven hair that shadowed his face.

Aldred.

Suddenly there was light, brilliant and blinding white. Noise too – like the thunder-crack of passing-through. And in that instant, with no logical explanation whatsoever, young Tom Summerville was by the *side* of the road and the car was gone. Gone, as if it had never been there at all. Save for the misty swirl of blue spat from the exhaust pipe.

Kill me. He tried to kill me...

And hadn't that –

Tom swallowed hard and realized his hands were clenched almost white. He relaxed them a little and the ache that had started up his forearm eased.

– hadn't that fat red sports car been in town the day of the accident?

... the way he killed my parents. And everyone else like me. All the Descendants from the world I know. Voices. Grey. Distant. "Go on and you will d—"

"Tom... Tom, are you OK?"

Panicky fast Tom turned, tightly grabbed the jacket of his frowning friend and looked him hard in the eyes.

"Doug ... Douglas, I don't want you to

come with me. When we reach the Subway I want you to stay here."

"On my own?"

"No. The old man will be with you."

"But I don't want to stay with him, Tom. I don't even know him."

"He won't harm you," Tom said firmly, working hard not to give way to Douglas's expression of hurt bewilderment.

"But, Tom, I—"

"Douglas," Tom snapped. "I'm going alone."

A stony silence fell, long, cold. Then Douglas's words came so softly that Tom could barely hear them.

"You're ditching me?"

Douglas's bewildered expression had changed. Now it was plain hurt. Tom had to turn away. No, he thought, I'm not ditching you, Doug. I'm scared for you. I don't want to see you harmed.

"Yes," said Tom. "I'm ditching you."

They silently ate the food Aaron produced from the sack he'd been carrying. It was fruit mostly, and grill-browned discs of a doughy substance that tasted a little like salty pancakes. There was also a large bundle of purplish meat sticks and several cubes of something like bright green Turkish delight. These, both boys politely but firmly declined.

Five hours later, five hours and fifteen aching miles of hills and dips, fords and fences, old and new (at one point they passed a towering white-brick windmill which was bathed in an eerie glow from a lone standing, pointlessly lit, streetlamp) and they had reached the mouth of the cave; at the base of the hill with the tunnel cut through it.

The Subway.

Aaron lowered himself onto one of the large concrete blocks that peppered the entrance of the Subway. Tom wearily sat up against the main concrete pillar at the mouth of the tunnel, his heart beating fast: It was dark in that Subway cave. Very dark indeed. Beside him, Douglas stood gaping into the blackness and considered that maybe it was not such a bad idea for him to stay this side after all.

The next five minutes were a dizzying whirl of instructions, commands and warnings. A lot of which Tom couldn't begin to understand: Don't do this ... avoid that ... dusk is best and keep to the path through the Pitch Forests... Take this, and put on these. You won't stand out so much.

From his canvas sack Aaron pulled a hide bag that looked to Tom like one of his aunt's old leather scatter cushions but with added carry strap and a spout sticking out of one corner, and a string-tied bundle of crumpled rags: grey jeans that were very baggy and gathered at the ankles like the pants of a pierrot clown, a once white but now damp-stained collarless shirt with similar loose and baggy sleeves, and a dirty, tan leather waistcoat which smelt of all the foul animal smells Tom had ever encountered – and worse.

Finally Aaron handed Tom the key.

"Why are you doing this?" asked Tom as he took the key. "Did you work for the Old King? Were you his stableman or something?"

After a moment in which Aaron seemed to recall a thought from a brighter time, he said, "I was Lord Nightshade, his friend and councillor. We drank a whole ale barrel dry the day Tyso was born, and later when the king travelled, I was the boy's tutor in ways of astrology and physic."

"You don't look like a lord," Douglas said with a quiet honesty that bothered Tom a little.

"That," murmured the old man, "is good." Tom slipped into the rags Aaron had handed him, discarding, a little reluctantly, his own comfortable jacket and jeans. The old man had also produced from his bag a pair of incredibly heavy and odd-looking calf boots which Tom smartly suggested might slow him down, choosing instead to kick up a little of the dark earth and rub it into his own shoes to make them less noticeable.

That was ten minutes ago.

Now it was dark. Earlier there had been some light – not much, but enough for Tom to make out the paved ground, the skeleton of overhead iron rafters and the heavy concrete pillars that lined the Subway walls.

But now the blackness was complete.

Now Tom was a million miles from home.

Now something indescribably hideous could brush past his shoulder, or steal up behind him in this dismal tunnel that echoed with the sound of his pounding heart and the silvery ringing of dripping water, and he would never know until it was all too late.

The shirt Aaron had given him was coarse but Tom hardly felt the terrible itching it ought to have caused. He was busy counting steps. But only in his head.

Eighty-four … eighty-five…

Not too fast.

Eighty-six … seven…

Not too slow.

Eighty-eight … eighty-nine…

And try not to think–

Ninety.

–about the terrible things that might be clinging to the walls … hanging from the rafters … slithering underfoot …

Keep moving: Ninety-one. Ninety-two.

… spinning enormous webs as strong as fishing nets across the…

STEALING UP BEHIND YOU.

Tom stopped: A noise, behind.

Shuffling.

And then it was gone, either never there at all, or drowned by the swelling sound of water, dripping, sloshing. Tom swallowed hard and continued forward. For most parts the ground was still dry (though it had lost the firmness of the concrete at the entrance) but occasionally Tom wandered into a soggy pothole full of syrupy liquid that ran over his shoes and made the thought of Aaron's Frankenstein boots a little more bearable.

Ninety-nine. One hundred.

And Tom froze. That shuffling was back. Louder this time, and panting with it. Deep, like that of a big dog.

And it was close.

Tom wished Douglas were with him. But only for a moment. Because suddenly that panting grew louder and hoarse, close and closer, and Tom was glad that Douglas was back there, safe.

If he were to die here – now – Aaron would take care of Douglas. Only this thought comforted Tom at this black moment when terror, real terror, not the assumed kind of big school bullies and not-so-dark windswept alleys, was absolute.

Except that it wasn't; not quite. Not yet.

The terror became absolute only when the animal-thing behind reached out and laid five damp, death-cold fingers on his neck.

And in this terrible moment when Tom felt both fever-hot and freezing cold, the thing spoke.

Or at least seemed to.

"Tts ... tsssssohhh ... ohhh."

It sounded pained, breathless.

"Waa ... waaii ... wai ... ttthhhh."

And perhaps a little ... scared.

"Wai ... Tom ... wait."

And a little like...

"Wait for me, Tom. Don't go, please."

No. Not a little. A lot like ... "Douglas?"

Tom slowly turned. He could see nothing in front of him. He could see nothing of himself except a very faint ghost of his white shirt.

"Douglas?"

"I'm sorry, Tom. I got scared. This place is so ... strange. I didn't want to be here without you."

Douglas had rushed the words out. Now he broke off to catch his breath. Tom became wary of the silence, aware of the dark again.

"Doug?" he reached out and Douglas shrieked at his touch.

"Oh, Tom. Don't do that. Not in a place like this. You scared the life out of me."

"Sorry, Doug," Tom said quickly. And then he sighed, not sure yet if he was relieved or angry.

"You left this. I thought you might need it."

Tom could not see what Douglas was talking about, but a moment later he felt his friend touch his shoulder, run his hand along to his arm, to his hand, take it and close his fingers over the forgotten item. It was his father's gun. Tom could tell it blindfold. It was so comfortable in his hand it might have been specially forged for him. The pistol, even though its spring was now weak and contained just one small .22 calibre pellet, made Tom feel a little more capable. With his free hand, Tom grabbed the arm of Douglas's jacket.

"Doug," he began as positively as he could, "I want you to go back."

And Douglas said, "No."

There were several ways in which Douglas said "No", Tom had learned over the years. There was the Well, I don't really want to but if you honestly think I should **no**.

The I don't know, Tom. Maybe you're right no.

And occasionally, only occasionally, there was the *Tom, you could force burning matchsticks under my fingernails and you still won't get me to change my mind* no.

This present no belonged strongly to the latter.

And so, tremblingly cautious, Tom holding on to Douglas, Douglas clutching at Tom, slowly and silently they started forward.

The blackness remained total and the

ground had developed a slight downward slant. *Journey to the Centre of the Earth*, Tom thought uneasily, as water sloshed under their feet and turned the ground into paste. Fifteen minutes later, still following a downward path as dark as a sealed coffin, that uneasiness had turned to real worry. With every new step a new "what if" surfaced. But they continued forward. Douglas following Tom. Tom going forward because Douglas kept with him.

Some time later, the dripping ceased and the ground was beginning to change. Slosh turned to doughy clay. Doughy to firm. Firm became hard. And now that hardness had crumbled away to dust. It felt like walking over sand-dunes in the dead of a moonless night.

Only there was a moon.

Douglas stopped.

"Look, Tom, look."

Except that it wasn't.

But it was light. A faint, pinprick of yellow. The end of the Subway.

Tom became aware of the changes in the Subway as the first glimmers of light began to filter their way in. It was still the Subway, the wide man-made tunnel it had been at its Far-posts entrance, but here, close to its exit, there was no sign of the modern iron rafters, the huge concrete pillars or the even slabs of Far-posts paving. There *were* pillars, just as huge, propping up the shaft, but these were nothing more than roughly cut tree trunks. Equally basic were the wooden beams and rafters, and the dust of the mid-section had run away to small, black stone cobbles.

The atmosphere had changed too. It was no longer warm and humid. It was hot, dry.

Tom licked his lips. "Almost there," he whispered, and then wondered if Douglas had noticed the apprehension he felt in his throat.

Almost there, Doug. Just a few more steps and we'll know what's out there.

6

HEAT AND HUNGER

"Desert?" Douglas gasped.

Brightness ahead, a screaming mouth of blackness behind, both boys stood squinting as hot wind, like warm fingers, brushed back their hair.

It wasn't quite a desert, but it was perhaps the closest thing to it. A rolling plain of sunbleached earth, freckled here and there with tiny islands of coarse yellow grass, and occasionally – only occasionally – a tall and twisted tree similar to the terrible oak they had encountered at their entrance to the Farposts.

Tom scanned the area. There were no buildings in sight. No landmarks. Simply wasteland in every direction.

Switching the waterbag from left shoulder to right, Tom felt the prickling heat at his neck and remembered the first of the old man's instructions.

Keep the sun to your back and follow your heart.

So, after throwing a brief glance behind, the two boys – one in training shoes, denim jeans and bright blue ski-jacket, the other in old, ill-fitting rags – together set out across the wasteland.

Tom brushed hair, darkened with sweat, out of his eyes. The sun was higher now, hotter. He had discarded his waistcoat on a bank of a dried-up stream several miles back, but still wore the itchy shirt Aaron had given him as protection against the sun's rays. Douglas too had shrugged off his ski jacket but still carried it responsibly around his waist the way he would have back home in Greenvale. Now his sweatshirt was equally patched with areas of damp and dry.

The boys had been walking for two hours or more.

The wasteland of the last few miles had recently given way to sparse-covered fields of heather and occasional patches of wheat – similiar to the tall stalks encountered in the Farposts, except that here it was wilting and sun-scorched. When you pushed through it the brittle stalks snapped rather than yielded.

Tom judged they had travelled eight, perhaps

nine hard miles. Now they rested in the shade of an ancient windmill. It was similar, Tom thought, perhaps even identical, to the windmill of the Farposts, except that this one was lit only by the scorching sun, not some inappropriate street lamp.

As Tom sat against Douglas and took a first cautious sip of the warm sweet water from the hide bag Aaron had given him, a thought began to turn.

Windmills and street lamps ... asphalt and cobbles.

"Now I know why the Farposts was so strange."

"Uh?" Douglas replied. He was staring up at the windmill's sails. Their tattered coverings were flapping in the hot wind like holiday bunting. "Why?"

"The Farposts is a middle world, Doug. See, there's Greenvale and Edonia. Greenvale is Greenvale. Edonia is Edonia. But the Farposts is both. That's why it could have hot-dog vans and gallows and windmills together."

Tom handed the bag to his friend. Douglas surveyed it warily, rubbed his chin with more care than usual and looked the question at Tom.

"Well, it tastes pretty weird but I think it's safe."

Douglas appeared unconvinced. His nose wrinkled in the suspicious fashion typical of

the old Doubtful Douglas Tom knew so well.
He sniffed the bag's nozzle, poured a little of
the tinted liquid onto his hand and after eyeing
it warily, took a sip. After a further pause he
took another. Then another. And another. A
gulp. A guzzle. Then...

Tom yanked the bag away.

"Hey, go easy with that. It may have to last
us a long time."

"A *long time*?" Douglas's eyes widened.

"Only maybe." Tom hastily added, deciding
to keep his worries to himself.

*Nine miles and nothing so far but dead
wheat and a few scorched-out buildings. We
could be a million miles from anywhere, Doug.
But you don't want to know that, do you? You
don't want to think about how long it might
take to starve to death, or whether the water
will run out first. Wonder what you're thinking now. Hope you're not regretting it too.*

"Tom, are we lost?"

They had travelled another five or six miles.
The sun was low and red now, painting their
own shadows and those of the occasional
shrub all long and twisted.

Tom shrugged.

"How can you be lost when you never really
knew where you were to begin with?"

Other times Douglas might have debated the
question, or at least allowed pause for thought.

This time, however, he simply shrugged.

"But we are still heading in the direction we were told to go, so maybe over the next hill, Doug..."

Something hot rose in Tom's stomach and began to churn uncomfortably.

Maybe over the next hill...

Three hours ago Tom had truly believed that. An hour later doubts had begun to kick at his gut. Not long after, his aching legs, parched lips and sunburned neck said that maybe the old man had got it wrong; that the Pitch Forests and the Dark Tower in which Prince Tyso was imprisoned were in another direction completely. Now that *maybe* had changed to *probably*; after all, everything Aaron had said had been so vague: "Keep the sun to your back and follow your heart." What the heck kind of instruction was that?

So here they were, both boys shambling on in their own silent thoughts. Exhaustion setting in. Their tired feet barely lifting off the dusty ground.

So the old man had got it wrong. Tom scanned the parched wasteland in every direction and truly believed it. Soon he would have to tell Douglas, but for the moment they carried on, deep in their own dark thoughts.

More than two hours later nothing had changed, except that the aches had got worse and the peppery dust had turned their throats painfully raw. Now and then they stopped to run a hand over their dusty eyelids, but dryness forbade crying. Ten minutes later there was a smudge of grey on the horizon.

The Pitch Forests.

And darkness was coming.

They spent the night in an abandoned cabin, found after another blistering mile. Like everything in this land it was very simple: just a small log-built shack that possessed one roughly crafted timber table and bench seat. There were two earthenware bottles and one darkwood bowl on the table, but the bottles were empty and whatever fruit had been in the bowl had long since withered to something that now resembled oversized green-skinned prunes that filled the dim space with a sickly smell of decay.

Yet they endured it.

True, it was unpleasant, but perhaps, they decided, safer than spending the night out there in the dark.

Sighing, Tom threw the bowl of dead fruit far into the night and, sitting up against the bench on which Douglas lay restlessly turning, he began to think about home, about all the boys in Greenvale that night who would be sitting down to warm suppers in comfortable rooms. He thought of Aunt Jess and wished he were there, safe.

It was a long time before Tom Summerville slept that night.

Heat and hunger woke him. Tom knew almost instantly where he was; the hard stone of the floor in no way belonged to his comfortable bedroom, his rough peasant shirt was not his soft pyjama top. After that everything came back fast.

Stirring sleepily he licked his lips and put a hand to his stomach. How long had it been since he had last eaten?

He stretched awake, wincing at the aches the hard night on the stone had caused, while the question reached his drowsy mind, turned there a moment and then was gone. For something hit the floor near Tom with a thud and startled it away.

Tom jumped.

He squinted down at the thing before him as the morning sun, cutting a thick yellow wedge through the dust of the open doorway, revealed it.

It was a small package, slightly shiny, black and red and crumpled at one end. Gradually, Tom's eyes focused.

Red letters: M-A ...

Dark surround.

Gold edging: R-S ...

M-A-R-S.

A Mars bar. A good old-fashioned chocolate-coated Mars bar. Or at least part of one.

Homesickness came again in a painful wave. Tom had to push it to the back of his mind.

In the darkest corner of the shack something stirred. But it was only Douglas, looking awake – alert. He looked to Tom's eyes as if he had been awake a long time – or hardly asleep at all.

"It's a bit squishy because of the heat, but I figured you'd want some anyhow."

Pulling himself into a cross-legged position in the centre of the cabin, Tom smiled at Douglas's innocent knack for stating the obvious. It made him think of similar moments in less troubled times.

"Thanks, Doug."

"'s OK. I found it in my inside pocket. I bought it for the park yesterday but after … well, you know, after everything that happened, I forgot about it."

Tom couldn't restrain a beam of pride. Doug must have woken up starving too and if he wanted to could have finished the sweet without Tom's ever knowing. Instead, stuck in this dismal shack, miles from anywhere, he chose to share it.

"Thanks," Tom said again, and thoughtfully chewing the tasty chocolate bar he pulled the key from the pouch at this belt and wondered what might be yet to come. Then he remembered the Scroll. He had given it to

Douglas to keep safely inside the zipper pocket of his jacket. Doug now handed it to him.

Go through a tunnel deep and grave...

"That must have been the Subway," said Douglas. "That was grave. We've passed that part."

Then over fields that once raised seed.

"And these," Tom waved towards the open doorway, "must be the fields. We've been passing dried up patches of wheat for miles, haven't we?"

Douglas nodded. Tom read the next line silently. Dropping down beside him, Doug looked at it too.

To where the trees and giants feed.

Tom quickly rolled up the Scroll and gave it back to Douglas. Then, leaving the cabin to bake in the heat of a cloudless afternoon, they set off once more.

Up ahead the Pitch Forests looked like a solid wall of blackness, they were so dark and dense. And they were whispering. But of course that was impossible. Just wind whistling through the undergrowth, Tom told himself.

Just wind, Douglas thought likewise. *Don't be silly. Trees don't whisper.*

And all the time they were drawing closer, and closer.

*　　*　　*

Aldred was drawing closer too. But it was a full day later that he, astride a fine black stallion and trailed by five Knights of the New Order, reached the Pitch Forests. The men following Aldred were not real knights at all; all the old Edonian knights had been killed several years earlier. These New Order Knights were simply criminals – murderers mostly – set free from the dungeons of Edonia when Aldred was gaining power over the land. Their number was not great, for there were few truly evil men in Edonia. Perhaps there were eighty "knights" all told. Most of them were stationed at Crestoban Castle now that Prince Tyso, its rightful occupant, had gone.

The knights kept a respectful distance as Aldred drew his horse to a stop before the trees. Being so close to the dark, whispering forest made the horses uneasy. One began to paw fretfully at the ground. Another, like Tom's clockwork lancer, reared up and almost threw its rider.

"Why do we stop?" asked the leading knight, a burly, red-beared man clad in a dull leather tunic which was striped with grey metal plates at the shoulders and elbows.

Aldred did not look round. "Perhaps the boy is already dead. The forests can be treacherous even to those who know them well. But we cannot take the chance. Tom Summerville may have a little magic of his own."

Hanging from the lowest branch of the tree Aldred had stopped before was a horn. It was like a horn from a Viking helmet, streaked light brown to dark and edged with the same grey metal as the knights wore. Aldred plucked it down, raised it to his thin dark lips, and blew.

Not long after the blaring note faded there came a scurrying sound from the shadows between the trees. A shadow darted among the leaves, then a trace of whiteness appeared – a deathly white face quite low to the ground. It moved closer in an odd, scuttling motion, but stopped before the shadows ended, as if the bright sunlight outside might somehow harm it.

The silence was broken by a sharp, rasping sound as the dark barrel of a rifle appeared through the leaves: one of the guns Aldred himself had offered the Forest People on his first journeys northward. One of his bribes.

"Put away the rifle," he hissed. "It is I, Prince Aldred."

The rifle hastily withdrew.

"The Outlander boy has entered your woods. Take a band of your finest men and bring him to me. He is travelling north, towards the Greyland Prairies."

A terrible slurping sound came from the leaves and a moment later the creature, in an odd voice that would have been difficult for strangers to understand, said, "And whersh, Your Highnesshh, will we finds you when we have the childshhh?"

"We are travelling north along the eastern edge of the land. Three sundowns from now we shall have reached the High Cliffs of Rynn. See that you bring him there."

"Alive," asked the Forest creature, "orsh dead?"

If Aldred replied the creature did not hear it. He had pulled his horse round and started on the long journey around the Pitch Forests.

"Keep to the path, Tom. Keep to the path…"

It was an old man's voice. Aaron's shaky drawl that kept turning over in Tom's head like a stuck record running a fraction too slowly.

"Keep to the path through the Pitch Forests…"

But it wasn't easy. It was so dim in there. The trees were so tightly bunched and their overhead branches so thickly matted, they let in very little light. Although it was daytime, it was like walking at twilight.

The path itself was far less impressive than Aaron had made it sound. Not, as Tom had imagined, some glistening, yellow-brick road, but simply a narrow line of broken paving almost completely overgrown in parts by strange-looking, knee-high plants that blanketed the area between the dark and oily-looking tree trunks. These plants, to Douglas's dismay, rustled frequently and occasionally spat up clouds of insects disturbed by some creature too small and too frightened to be seen. Often the path twisted and rose, and in the dips a milky, rotten-smelling mist hung in layers as thick as paint.

Tom led, kicking out here and there at an overgrown branch which had strayed onto the path, or flicking his hand at an oversized bug, beetle or some less familiar insect. Douglas, taking his turn carrying the waterbag, followed close behind, his jacket fastened at the throat in spite of the heat. At every rustle and crack, every whisper the trees let out, he nervously turned. Douglas didn't like this place. He hated it more than the terrible dark of the Subway and the awful closed-in feel and stench of the cabin, for this was the place of everyone's worst dreams. Being lost in the dark, alone and afraid. This was Hansel and Gretel for real.

Something buzzed at Douglas's ear. He shook his head wildly and then saw the insect, a black beetle the size of his own clenched fist, rise up and lose itself in the dim, shifting roof of the forest.

Doug's pace quickened. He ran into Tom, who had stopped to stare at something that could have been an animal form almost completely mummified in the wiry tendrils of the undergrowth.

"Oh, Doug. You nearly scared the pants off me."

"Tom … I don't like it here."

Tom slapped at his cheek and inspected the fat purple smudge the dead bug had left on his palm. He wiped it on his shirt. "I thought you liked it outdoors."

"Outdoors is fine. Out here's totally different."

Doug's voice was shaky. Tom's was calm, but it was hard to keep it sounding that way.

"Just think of this as one of Colonel Friedman's hikes out to Beverley. Remember the Outward Bound course? Least we won't starve. We'll eat up a tree root or skin a *wabbit*." As if it had heard, one of the trees creaked a gnarled bough. The noise it made sounded worryingly human – almost a gasp.

Tom noticed but did nothing.

Douglas heard and spun round fast.

"Tom, I just got attacked by the *biggest damn beetle* I ever laid eyes on. Now, if there are any rabbits here the chances are they're six feet tall and *they'll* skin *us*. That's if they don't simply swallow us whole!"

Tom reached a hand over his friend's shoulder, pulling him away from the decaying remains of another animal he'd just spotted cocooned in the vines of one of the shrubs, and he said with quiet honesty, "I'm sorry, Doug. I should never have got you involved in this."

Not far away something screeched and Douglas shivered. "It's kind of scary, isn't it?"

he said shakily. Then he thought for a moment and said, "Tom. I was wrong."

"Wrong?"

"When you asked me about those stories we sometimes read in your bedroom. Those adventure stories we found. I said I'd do it if I got the chance – but I lied. I only said what I thought you wanted to hear—"

Crack!

Back in the direction they came from. Another branch breaking. More rustling. More strange animal sounds.

Quickly, Tom grabbed Douglas and started them forward. The path turned and dipped sharply a little way ahead and at its lowest point the boys were more than waist deep in the thick, dank-smelling mist.

"You lied?" Tom said. "Just for me? Thanks, Doug. Thanks."

Tom's tone was sure as he moved them faster into the dark woodland: *We're going to make it, Doug,* he thought, *together we'll make it.*

Not long after this, things got worse.

7

WHERE THE TREES AND GIANTS FEED

"Tom... Tom, you hear that?"

"Hear what?"

"Exactly... A few minutes ago this place sounded like a zoo. Now listen."

Tom listened but heard nothing, except for that ghostly whispering he couldn't quite make out.

The noises had been bad. The quiet was worse.

Their pace quickened – until Tom stopped dead in his tracks. Up ahead the path broke into two.

Both paths were darker, narrower.

Both more overgrown than before.

Tom looked at Douglas. Douglas desperately looked back. And after only a moment's hesitation they took the left lane, because behind them, resonating through that strange whispering, another branch broke.

It didn't take Tom long to realize he had taken the wrong route. With almost every step the plants grew taller and thicker, and the over-head tangle of branches had become so tightly matted there was danger of losing what little light was left.

No more running; now the boys moved slowly and cautiously. The dark and mist had cut visibility down to ten feet at best and the path was narrower here, uneven, just one stone wide.

Douglas was gripping Tom's shirt so tightly it cut into his shoulder, but Tom didn't have time to complain. Suddenly, the whispering had stopped. And instantly both boys knew. Maybe some sixth sense more atuned to this world told them that something was wrong, or perhaps they simply felt the rumbling long before they heard it. Whichever, here it was now, a low pulsing in their stomachs as if, somewhere close by, a massive tanker from the world Tom Summerville knew better had revved its engine into life.

But of course it wasn't a tanker, for this was Edonia, not Greenvale. And the sound did not stem from some black-top carriageway to the left, right or straight on forward. It came from below. Directly below.

Tom felt it. Douglas almost screamed.

And IT, whatever IT might be, following the line of the hard-to-follow path, passed beneath them.

"Tom...?"

"I DON'T KNOW, DOUGLAS," Tom snapped. Then shame became greater than fear and he shook his head. More softly, he said, "I don't know, Doug. Maybe ... maybe it was some sort of earthquake or something."

"But—"

Douglas stopped.

Up ahead a paving stone moved, just a little sideways.

No, thought Tom. Just a trick of this trembling light. Then slowly, proving otherwise, one end of the rough, diamond-shaped slab began to sink into the ground as if something was clawing at it from below, while the end closest to the boys silently began to rise.

And from the dark beneath, just like the nursery rhyme, along came a spider. It was big – at least as big as the tarantula spider Douglas often liked to watch displayed in the downtown pet store back home. But this one was more akin to an ordinary house spider – a huge black angular house spider the size of Douglas Clayton's hand.

Tom gasped, and the spider, sensing it, tensed, sinking its dark body low, pulling its legs high and close – alert.

Douglas swallowed and dropped a reassuring

hand onto Tom's shoulder. Since before he could remember, Douglas had picked up ordinary house-spiders, played with them and then later, as a junior naturalist, kept them in jars and studied scientifically. They were old friends. He could run the biggest of them over his hands any time. They didn't scare him. This one did.

Tom, however, had never claimed a fondness for spiders and in truth he disliked them more than he ever admitted. Douglas knew this, though his friend had not actually said. It was plainly obvious the way colour would suddenly drain from his cheeks whenever one scurried across their path. Spiders were one thing Douglas never joked about; for in Tom's mind at least, they were too serious for that.

"Tom," whispered Douglas, trying to sound as positive as he could, "it's more scared of us than we are of it."

"Wa ... wanna bet?"

Douglas didn't answer, for out from the blackness beneath the diamond-shaped stone crawled another spider, even larger, half as big again. It looked at Tom – or at least in Tom's mind, seemed to – for a long, terrible time, and frozen in shock Tom could only gape back. Lost in this nightmare moment, he no longer saw the dark woods around him. He never heard the rustle of nearby leaves or the struggle that came soon after. Trapped in this nightmare sight he did not realize that Douglas had gone.

The first spider ran forward a foot or so, then stopped.

Tom lurched as if winded.

Now the other spider sprang to life, scurried ahead of its mate, and also stopped as if dead. Cunning as a spider.

Another harrowing scurry of legs and the first spider was close now. Perhaps two yards away. Maybe even closer. Without knowing it Tom crawled a hand up to his throat.

Tom backed off. Slowly now, together, the spiders crept forward.

One step. Two. Off the path and through the tangle of palmy growth which tore at his legs. And then he stopped: Towering tree behind, nightmare creatures ahead, there was no place left to go. Except...

Except forward. Fighting.

"Douglas," Tom whispered. Teeth and hands no longer shaking but clenched tight, ready. Louder, he repeated the call and finally allowed himself a quick sideways glance; for the spiders had stopped again.

"Doug—" Then something happened which made Tom tense so fast he bit his tongue and blood turned his mouth salty.

Both spiders moved at once. Not crawling slowly any more, but with a terrifying speed. House spiders are fast. These creatures were faster. Suddenly Tom remembered how to scream.

A wave of dizzying terror came, went, returned even stronger. But the spiders did not run for him as he feared they would; one spider ran left, the other disappeared into the grass to the right of the path.

In the shock and relief that followed, Tom hadn't realized that the rumbling was back.

As before he felt something thunder beneath him. Again he saw the paving-stones move. Yet this time it was different; for instead of just one slab rising with quiet, almost mechanical slowness, here a whole group of slabs moved together, exploding high into the air as if a powerful mine had been disturbed.

Instinctively Tom pulled his chin into his chest and shielded his head with both arms. Not much help, he had time to think glumly, if one of those big stone pieces comes crashing down his way. He hoped Douglas would come through it OK.

After the shower of paving, rubble and earth eased, Tom was relieved to find that all that had come his way was one apple-sized stone and about a sackful of earth – most of which was falling like a mini avalanche into his pants. Squirming to shake out the rubble, Tom looked around, and in the instant he noticed that Douglas was no longer beside him, he also realized that the oily trunk of the tree he had backed against now held him fast.

"Douglas?"

He looked into the shadows nearby.

Harder, he tried to pull away from the tree. Again he called.

But nothing moved. Nobody answered. There was a brief cracking sound as he pulled away from the tree, but then the effort of pulling became so great that Tom had to give in to the tree and pause for rest.

"I'm stuck, Doug. Help me, please."

But somehow Tom knew that Douglas wouldn't reply. Not now. Not after – how long – two? five? ten minutes? In here, in shock, it was hard to tell. There was a large, new-formed crater up ahead but Douglas was not there. Tom knew this because he had barely taken his eyes from it since it was created.

Then there was movement from the darkness inside the crater.

Of course he could have been wrong.

Please, Tom thought. Let me be wrong. Make it be Douglas crawling out, safe. Coming to free me.

But it wasn't Douglas. It was another spider. Or at least, for the moment, part of one. Just its front legs crawling for purchase at the base of this deep dark hole not more than ten yards away. One of the spider's legs scratched into the dirt at the left side of the hole while its other front leg twitched the ground far to the right.

Three feet! Tom thought. *From toe to toe*

those legs are at least three feet apart. That means that ... that the monster down there must be at least the size of—

The legs found their purchase.

Tom felt a spear of terror slice through him.

Again he tried to pull away from the tree but fear had turned his head light and drained all power from his body.

Please, God, he thought, *if this is a nightmare, end it now.*

The spider moved fast. In one nervous scurry it was out of the hole, facing Tom and starting slowly forward as it pumped its spit-shiny mandibles (or was that blood?) in, out, in, out, in, out...

And it spoke.

Except that in his confusion Tom had got it wrong. There was a voice – but not the spider's.

Squeeze, Tom...

His father's voice. Softly, in his head.

Don't pull the trigger, Tom, squeeze it.

The gun! His pistol. In the terror he had forgotten. Now, with an almighty cry Tom yanked his left arm free. Fumbling, he grabbed the gun from his waist and raised it towards the approaching monster. And then, with the knowledge that if this one feeble pellet didn't kill the spider the first time, then at least soon it would be over – he *squeezed* the trigger.

Once.

Twice.

And nothing happened except that the spider got closer; so close that Tom thought he could see his helpless reflection a thousand times over in the spider's glistening black eyes. Then everything came at once: the sound, the light, the heat.

It took Tom two hard blinks and the first scorching wave of air to realize what had happened. That this time it was no tiny FLY-RITE pellet that shot from the gun barrel, but some unseen energy that on reaching its target engulfed it in a crackling ball of flame.

The same immense power Aldred had fired at Tom that night in the lane, only now it had come from Tom himself.

Tom pulled the gun tight to his chest, for the moment able to do nothing but gape at the burning spider. Then another stinging wave of heat fanned out with one last spider-scream and he had to turn – as best he could. The glue of the tree trunk still held him, but the waves of warmth were loosening it. By the time the creature had collapsed into a heap of dying embers Tom was drenched in sweat and almost free.

Two slow, sluggish strides later – like wading through deep water, Tom had time to think – and the final finger of glue broke. Most slapped back at the tree, quick to merge again, ready for another chance at some not-so-wilful prey. The few stubborn strands still clinging to the coarse weave of Tom's shirt thrashed back fast. They stung, the way a close-fired rubber band did, but Tom could live with the soreness. At least he was free.

Yes. Now he had time to ponder the situation.

He was free. The spider was dead. And Douglas was gone.

Not missing. Tom knew. Not dead.

But gone.

Now time seemed almost to stop. Minutes stretched into hours.

Hours became like days.

For three exhausting hours Tom combed the area in a dizzying spiral, calling Douglas until his throat stung and his voice trailed away to nothing more than a whisper. Until he was lost and angry, thorn-cut, nettle-stung and weak. Until he had become so tired he was no longer frightened and too exhausted to cry any more.

Finally, in a rocky clearing between the trees where the crisp plants had crumbled away to dust, he dropped against the largest boulder and, pulling himself as small as possible, he buried his head in his arms and cried.

Tom woke with a start. Something that looked like a huge stingray fish flapped overhead with a puzzling slowness and a cry that sounded like a scream from a horror film.

He stirred out of the hunched position he had found himself in and looked around. He was no longer up against the largest rock in the centre of the clearing but in a shaded hollow at the side of it. And, he noticed with momentary dismay, he was covered in leaves and branches and mouldy grass.

But he himself had done this, he now recalled, during the night after starting out of some awful dream. He had done it for protection – camouflage – not because it had been cold. For this place, Edonia, was never cold; sometimes late at night there was a breeze that rumoured coolness but that was only in comparison to the blistering temperatures of midday. No, usually Edonia was hot – often it was scorching.

Now, as the early morning sun cut bars of light through the dust between the trees, it *was* hot, Tom's brow was already blistered with sweat and he was thirsty. Very thirsty indeed. Or so he thought at the time.

Around four hours, and perhaps the same number of miles, later, Tom realized that he had not been thirsty – a little, maybe more than a little dry perhaps, but not really thirsty.

Now he was. But he tried not to think about it. In fact, as he continued wearily through the forest he tried not to think about anything at all. The facts were so scary.

No food. No water. Douglas gone. Himself lost.

But...

But at least Douglas had the waterbag. Wherever he was, he wouldn't die of thirst. Not for some time anyway.

He rested at midday and started walking again just as drowsiness was creeping over him. He didn't like to sleep in the forest. It brought bad dreams of man-eating plants and monstrous creatures watching him from the shadows with terrible, strangely clever eyes.

The further he travelled, the slower he went.

His feet were burning, his throat was on fire and he was so dry he couldn't swallow. Earlier, in desperation, he had broken a stalk from one of the yellowy rhubarb-like plants that grew around the base of the trees and bitten into the slightly moist flesh. It was the bitterest thing he had ever tasted. It felt like acid on his tongue.

He threw the stalk away and kept on walking, hoping that the forest would suddenly end and there would be a cool, clear lake in which to bathe and drink.

But the forest didn't end.

Maybe five minutes, an hour, six hours later (Tom wasn't sure about time any more, the drowsiness was back and now there was no way to shrug it off) he dropped to his knees and closed his eyes. He would sleep now, sleep long and deep and if he happened to wake next day he would try and go on. If he didn't wake up – well, at least he had tried. Nobody could—

Crick!

Tom forgot about dying in an instant. Close by, one of the terrible forest animals stirred among the dark shadows.

It sounded big.

Fumbling for the gun at his belt, Tom started slowly back to a safer, more shaded area several yards behind. In his mind spun dizzying pictures of giant spiders with mouths like ancient mantraps. Yet strangely, even though his heart was racing, his pace remained even. He didn't panic the way he might have done only a week ago when he was plain Tom Summerville, the schoolboy from Greenvale, who knew nothing of survival and fear. Now he realized that certain situations were too grave for panic.

Slowly Tom backed towards the shadows – calmly, cautiously and in silence. In silence, that is, until a tendril from one of the low-growing palms spat out like a coiled-up tongue, lashing his ankle and making him falter. Tom cried out, half aloud, and then, remembering the monster in the dark, half stifled, as he swayed to find balance, leaning forward, then back, looking like a high-wire artist in danger of falling...

And fall Tom did. Balance gone, back he

toppled, striking his head against something much taller and harder.

It was a tree. One of the oily, fat-rooted trees that could only exist in a place as ghastly as the Pitch Forests. His right arm, which had flung out in the tumble, was raised above his head, held by the flypaper surface of the bark as if nailed there. To any casual onlooker it might have seemed as if he were waving.

And five feet away – glinting in the grass like a penny far down a grating covered with too fine a mesh – his gun.

Pounding: But only in Tom's heart. He could hear it clearly now, for the thing in the shadows had fallen silent. Probably, Tom thought bitterly, waiting to see if I'm really stuck. Licking its lips or mandibles or whatever it has, working up an appetite. The nightmare picture that suddenly flashed in Tom's head spurred him into action. Deep breath taken, hand fisted tight, he pulled his arm from the tree. One inch. Two. Perhaps three powerful, muscle-shaking inches, then back it snapped. And, as if this were a familiar signal of submission, the monster in the shadows stirred from its watchful position ahead and sidled round the thicker growth, closer.

Oh yes, it *was* big. Tom could see from its dark, fast-moving outline. Almost as big as Tom himself. Just like the spider it was *big* and *smart* and *cautious* and *cunning*. And it was stealthy too – for one moment it was there, the next it was gone.

But of course, it hadn't gone. Not really. It simply waited in the shadows, *watching*.

The next few minutes passed with schoolroom slowness. All the time Tom working at his stuck-fast hand while looking here and there, but mostly to the spot, left, where IT had last been seen.

And then he turned and there IT was, so near he could touch it. Close but still cautious; silently studying Tom as if *he* were the strangest creature of all in a land too full of them.

And Tom gaped too, because for him this sight was more unexpected here, in the thick of the forest, than a giant spider or a strange flying fish in no need of water to keep it afloat. It was a boy. No taller than himself. No older than himself.

Just a boy.

Except this boy was different from Tom Summerville and other boys from more familiar places. Then Tom – stuck, going nowhere – allowed himself a closer look and realized. No. Not different. It was just that his military-looking clothes of faded red tunic with dull yellow braiding, and the green and brown patches smudged across his face like paratrooper's camouflage paste, made him appear different. This, and his raven black hair and same coloured eyes. The soft, peaceful eyes of a seal cub set in the round, open face of a boy. At the boy's belt, a pistol, something akin to an old flintlock, nested in a brown leather holster, while at his opposite side a small red drum hung easily at his hip.

The boy's right hand held tightly the drumsticks.

His left twitched nervously close to the gun.

And he was watching Tom warily. As warily as Tom was watching him. Tom wished Douglas were here. He'd know what to do.

"You just gonna sit there?" he'd yell. "Get yourself shot?"

"Come on, Tom," would be his father's reply. "You can do it, can't you?"

Maybe...

One last try then. Tom pulled his arm forward, leaning all his weight into it until his entire body trembled and something in his jaw cracked.

As before, the glue holding his arm stretched an inch, two, three ... and this time more, perhaps eight inches all told before snapping back at the rough bark with a powerful crack that sent dull pain throbbing up to his fingertips and water to his eyes.

No heat from a burning spider to loosen its tack this time, Tom thought glumly, and then groaned – as much from anguish as from the pain which burned his hand. He looked up at the boy. At his outcry the boy had backed off and pulled the gun from its holster. Now he ran the back of his drumstick hand across his mouth and squinted ... cautiously ... warily ... distrustfully? Silence then. Long. Watchful. The boy studying Tom. Tom thinking of anything to do, try, say, and nothing coming.

Then, "Help?"

Not Tom's voice. Not Douglas's in his head. But the drummer boy's.

And Tom, after a long moment of numbed surprise, quietly nodded.

8

SILAS

The drummer boy cut Tom free and handed
him his gun. He spoke Tom's language – or at
least a pidgin form of it. His name was Silas
and he was twelve harvests old. Silas did not
live in the Pitch Forests – "By the Gold Star,
no!" He had shrieked at Tom's question in
such an excitable way that Tom immediately
thought of Douglas.

No, the boy continued more calmly. He
simply used the Forests as a place to hide when
the knights who followed the false prince were
close. Of course the Forests were dangerous,
but not as dangerous as Aldred and his followers, and there were ways to survive. This
time Silas wasn't hiding, he was travelling
north through the Forests in search of the
Resistance – a band of fighters loyal to the true
prince. He had heard that they were in the

Northern Territories and Silas wished to join them in their fight.

Tom learned these facts as he followed the boy northward.

Maybe the Resistance would have news of Douglas. Maybe Douglas was with them.

Silas moved fast through the trees, dodging and weaving among the thick undergrowth with the skill of someone who had done it often.

In hope of slowing his new friend's pace a little, Tom said, "I'm looking for the Dark Tower, Silas. Do you know it?"

Halfway over the skeleton of a fallen tree, the boy stopped, grabbed an up-pointing bow and turned.

"The Darks Tower?"

Tom paused a moment, then nodded. "Yes."

Silas sucked in a chestful of air. "Bads," he whispered. "The place where the wrong thoughts come from. Aldred turned the Tower's thoughts bad and caused the water to stops falling."

Tom was suddenly aware of the dryness in his throat again. He scanned the area but saw no sign of the moist but bitter stalked plants of earlier. Here there was only thin fern, its dark stems as narrow and brittle as drinking straws.

"How could Aldred stop the water falling?"

"The power of the Olds King is strong. He stole the power from the true prince. When he firsts came to challenge the prince our land was green and fulsome. Farms was busy, the graingrass was talls and yellow."

Just like the fields in the Farposts – the thought struck Tom.

"After the last king died Aldreds tried to win the hearts of the people with bad talks – lies. He turned the Nomad Tribesfolk against the Fieldworkers. For twelve seasons they fought. Somes, in the Farcorners, still do. But mostly the Inner Wars ended when the Pacts were signed."

"Then what happened?"

"The first droughts come five harvests past. First, peoples continued to fight. But with less and less cloudwater there was no real hope. Crops failed. Foods got short. Most now serves the false prince in the Northlands, where they say water is got from an underground spring."

"How do others get water?" asked Tom.

"They haves to dig – deep down in the ground. But even the deepest holes are beginning to dry ups."

They walked a while further, then rested in the shade of a huge slab of white fungus which angled out from the ground like a flat outcrop of rock Tom remembered from a geology book he had once scanned. Tom thought of that book and the school library in which he had found it. Right then it seemed so far away as to be almost a dream.

Movement distracted his thoughts. Silas, by his side, was reaching up to the soft grey underside of the fungus, sinking his fingers in and pulling away a cricketball-sized chunk. To Tom's surprise, instead of tossing it from hand to hand or throwing it away, as if it were a fine ripe peach, Silas then bit a huge chunk out of it. Just as surprisingly he took a second bite, chomping it down and smacking his lips. On the third fast, enormous bite – obviously the table manners of Tom's world hadn't found their way to Edonia – Silas caught Tom gawping.

"Is there something wrong, Tom?"

Tom looked into Silas's dark eyes, then shook his head and just as Silas had done, reached up to the roof of the fungus. It seemed he no longer understood right and wrong.

But, what the heck; he'd chewed his way through foul-smelling roots that looked like dried-up octopus legs and crunched bitter-tasting, rhubarb-like stalks until he was sick. This oversized piece of mushroom could hardly be worse.

So … an apple-sized ball of the grey-white fungus in his left hand, a poisonous hank of bitter steel wool in his mind, Tom took a bite. And it tasted…

So unlike its appearance the effect was startling, like an optical illusion. Real but wrong. The flesh had a fruity, colourful tang not unlike ripe blackberries and the soft, fibrous texture of an overripe pear. But best of all, like that fruit it was wonderfully moist.

Just as Silas had done, Tom took a further two bites from the soft flesh and smacked his lips with a great self-satisfied slurp. Ten minutes later, pleasantly shaded and pleasantly full, Tom snuggled into the soft grass beneath the fungus, and quickly drifted into sleep.

And he dreamt. He dreamt of home. Of Greenvale and school. Of Douglas strangely in military tunic and even stranger camouflage paste, and Silas in jeans and modern day running shoes.

And he dreamt of a strange dark figure with fingers of fire and the rusty colour of hate in his eyes.

Tom came round with a strange rolling sensation in his head. Silas was leaning over him, rocking his shoulder.

"Tom! Tom, wake up, we've gots to go."

Groggy and dizzy, Tom shook the dream from his head, and something in his neck cracked. He winced.

Throwing a nervous glance into the dark growth to their left, Silas quickly laid two fingers over Tom's lips with a quiet shush. Tom's heart kicked up a beat. He didn't need to ask questions. What Silas said with his frightened expression and silent action was as telling as a roaring command.

Be quiet, Tom. There's danger. There's something out there and God help us if we're caught.

Rustling.

Grunting.

Something – no, Tom corrected himself – *many things,* by their sound, were cutting through the plant life close by. Tom pictured spiders again and suddenly a frightening urge to scream welled up in his throat.

Quietly, he moved up to see.

Four of them, with only a thin curtain of reedy stalks between, marched past, single file. Tom could feel Silas urging him down, but first he had to look again, even if only for a moment. For *they* had caught his eye and the effect was magnetic. In that heart-stopping moment Tom saw four, then six, eight, ten, then twelve flicker by in the lights and darks of the rustling leaves. At first, because of the dimness and the creatures' own nervous scur-ryings, it was hard to get a true picture. To begin with all Tom could make out was that they were bigger than the spider but smaller than himself. And then, the thing that had first caused him to look closer – that these creatures had the stature and same oddly round faces of garden gnomes. But joyless, leering gnomes from a nightmare garden with the chalk-white pallor of ghosts come midnight. And instead of cute little fishing-rods and safe-pointed picks, these monsters ran by with longbows and crossbows, gleaming swords and ... rifles.

Close now, closest, one of them, a rifle carrier with two munition belts crossing his broad chest like a Mexican bandit's, stopped. As if hearing the fear in Tom's heartbeat it turned, and peered into the reeds. So now Tom saw better. Saw the black dead-fish eyes, the damp, death-white skin and razor-toothed mouth pulled down at one side as if it were part of a white wax mask that this unbearable heat had caused to drip.

Tom groaned.

The creature leaned closer, the stubby fingers of its webbed hand tugging at the belt of bullets at his chest. Tom noticed its pointed fingernails and reached behind him. His hand found his gun easily, but in the same instant, Silas's hand closed firmly round it, saying – but only in his head – *No, Tom. Not yet. Maybe it hasn't seen us. Make a movement now and we will have the others to deal with.*

The next thing happened in an instant. With a low, liquid rumble, the gnome-thing drew its mouth into a dark lopsided O and fired a long green tongue at a bug the size of a golfball which had been hovering close to the roof of the fungus, so close to Tom that hot yellow spit caught his eye and he had to blink. For a moment he truly expected to be sick. But he wasn't and this horrendous incident broke the spell. He managed to look away, to pull himself smaller and deeper into the dark crease of the fungus, so close to Silas that the drummer boy's elbow dug sharp at this collar-bone. It ached, but Tom was glad to feel it there. Somehow it reassured him.

So now they lay still as statues. Just like the game he played with Douglas: statues. Move and you're dead. Blink and the monsters get you.

There was a horrible moment of garbled slurping after which the creature spat out the husk of the beetle. Then, after running the back of its hand across its mouth, it moved on. Four others followed it. Three creatures of its own kind and something bigger. Strange enough to make Silas himself risk a closer look. As it moved by them Tom, crouched low, managed only a glimpse of its feet, but that was all he needed. What else in the Pitch Forests would be wearing an old pair of size three tennis shoes? Tom had to stop himself from shouting.

"That's him," Tom whispered. "That was Douglas with those ... what are they?"

"Bad!" Silas frowned. "The Forest People were once friendlys. But that was the old time, before the drought turned the woodlands dry. Since Aldred tooks to the throne, everyone has changed. Even the clovecasters and weavemen are fighting over the Spire."

At other times Tom's curiosity might have led him to ask about the weavemen and the Spire, but at that moment he had more urgent things on his mind. Urgent, because although he was relieved at seeing Douglas again, what worried him was the fact that Douglas was not *walking* with these creatures.

Douglas's hands were fastened tightly behind his back, and he was being pulled along by the last two dwarfs. They were not pulling *gently*.

9

DANGERS IN
THE SAND

"Every steps I take, you follow," whispered Silas a few minutes later. They were following the Forest People, although they were now out of sight and Tom couldn't see how Silas was tracking them. They had turned off the path and Silas, turning here at a broken branch, there at an overturned stone, reminded Tom of a young Indian scout, from a film.

"What'll we do when we catch them?" asked Tom nervously as he reached the trunk of a fallen tree which Silas had easily hopped over.

Silas shrugged his shoulders and quickly had to flatten a hand over his drum as it rattled softly. "Forest Peoples are not so strong. They rests much. Sleep. We could surprise them. Steal one of their shooting sticks."

"I have a gun." Tom pulled the pistol from

the back of his pants and looked at it curiously. "But I've used it once already, and I'm not sure if it will work again. Maybe I should hold on to it."

They moved on, always keeping themselves close to the Forest People but just far enough back to be out of hearing range. Silas judged this, he told Tom, by the colour of the bruises on the trampled toadstools hidden among the tall grass. The bruises were dark yellow. If the toadstools had been kicked earlier they would have turned completely black. If the bruises were black then the Forest People would be so far ahead they would probably lose them.

Suddenly Silas slowed.

"What is it? Is there something wrong, Silas?"

More cautiously now, Silas led Tom on a little way further, then raised his hand for him to stop. They were standing before a bush with withered yellow berries hanging down in triangular bunches, like grapes. Tom thought Silas was going to pick the berries and surprise him with the taste as he had done with the fungus. But instead, Silas quietly peeled an opening in the branches and gestured to Tom to look between. There, in a dip below them, the Forest People had come to rest. They sat in three small groups. Douglas was among the largest group, still bound and fastened to the two ghastly dwarfs that had been pulling him earlier.

"If they've hurt Douglas," Tom, forgetting for the moment to be quiet, began. "I'll..."

Silas quickly shushed him with a frown which made the lines of camouflage paste on his brow ripple.

"But what can we do?" Tom asked, desperately.

"Now," Silas said as he placed his drum on the ground and shuffled into a comfortable sitting position on the grass next to it, "we waits!"

And wait they did.

Ten minutes. Twenty. Thirty. More.

For Tom at least, to stay silent and still so long was almost unbearable.

But as those long minutes ran towards an hour the Forest People, in ones and twos, slowly began to stretch and yawn and roll on to their sides. The snoring they made soon after was disgusting. Not much later, only one of the creatures remained awake. Even Douglas had begun to drowse in the heat.

"That one," explained Silas, "is the guard. It will not sleeps."

As if to confirm this, the remaining creature got to its feet and started to pace the length of the clearing, only changing direction to slurp occasionally from a grey metal tankard which rested on the top of a large boulder near to where Douglas lay.

*   *   *

"That is what stops the dreams coming," murmured Silas the next time it took a sip. "The drink is why he does not sleeps."

Tom considered what they might do. Although the guard was smaller than them, he did have a rifle. Perhaps they could distract him, or set a trap somehow. In truth, Tom wasn't hopeful of either suggestion. Traps took time to work out and distractions rarely worked.

Silas tapped Tom's shoulder and gave him the same silencing gesture as before. "Come with me, quietlys," he breathed before leading the way down towards the place where the Forest People slept.

Although it was only a short way down to the clearing, it took them some time to make it. They had to move slowly and quietly and only when the guard was pacing away from them. Each time he neared the bushy slope on which they hid, they stopped, Silas taking the opportunity during these stops to pick a handful of the yellow berries which hung from the lower branches of the bushes.

On reaching the bottom, Tom hardly dared breathe. Only a thin curtain of leaves separated them from the dwarves. The guard, back again to sip from the tankard, was so close that through the break in the bushes Tom could clearly see its dead white skin, blistered with sweat. Tom wondered if it could possibly hear his own heartbeat pounding in his chest.

The guard let out a terrible belch, clunked the tankard on to the rock and began pacing again.

Tom leaned closer into the bush. Douglas was no more than ten yards away. But that didn't mean much. However close Douglas was, they couldn't simply snatch him away. First they had to unfasten his bindings. To do this, Tom realized, they would have to deal with the guard. Maybe together, with Silas being fast and knowing the ways of these creatures, they could overpower him. With no other plan forthcoming, Tom decided to put the suggestion to Silas.

But Silas had gone. He had left his drum behind and was out in the clearing, dropping the freshly picked berries into the tankard. A green mist rose out and swirled around the rock as the berries dissolved. As if sensing something, the guard pulled the rifle from his shoulder, and turned.

Tom's heart leapt to his throat. But the mist had quickly thinned, and Silas, noticing the change in the creature's pacing, had ducked behind the rock. Tom could never have moved so swiftly. It it had been Tom out there instead of Silas, he would certainly have been caught.

The guard moved back to the rock like a cartoon character, its short legs running fast but carrying its fat little body only at a steady pace. As if a bad smell had drifted up from somewhere, it sniffed the air cautiously. It squinted at the tankard, then peered into the bushes close to where Tom stood.

Tom gripped the gun and curled his finger around the trigger. But then the guard turned, reaching its hand only a whisper away from where Silas crouched, and raised the tankard to its lips. It slurped the juice noisily, ran the back of its hand across its mouth and then something surprising happened. The creature, as Tom had expected, neither fell to the floor in pain from the poison nor slumped drowsily over the rock. But still holding the tankard, it froze. Really froze. Tom could see a thin layer of ice begin to glisten over its cheeks. The grey tankard it held was turning white with frost.

Quickly Silas beckoned Tom and together they set about untying Douglas. Silas worked at the bindings around Douglas's hands as Tom tugged at the twine around his feet. The vines the dwarves had used turned out to be so tightly fastened, however, that Silas had to steal one of the sleeping creatures' knives and cut Douglas free.

Douglas came round in stages, with a sleepy murmur as Silas was freeing his hands. Then, as Silas and Tom, one arm slung over each one's shoulder, dragged him out of the clearing, he began to gasp and twitch as if remembering a bad dream. And finally, as they made it back into the thick of the forest and his sleepy gaze settled on Silas with his shiny black eyes and his paint-smudged face, Douglas found his voice and shrieked himself awake.

It was Silas, not Tom, who managed to calm Douglas. He rooted out a core of leaves from one of the ground plants growing close to the trees, rolled them in his palms until blisters of juice drew to the surface, then swathed them over Douglas's sore wrists.

"Douglas be fines now." He nodded surely. And he was right. The leaves were as cool and soothing as any antiseptic could have been. The pain went almost immediately. For that Douglas was grateful. And shortly after this Douglas had something else to be grateful for. The end of the Forests.

It happened suddenly. There had been no signs to suggest change, so when it came, it was almost shocking.

Douglas was struck by the sky. It was grey – not an ordinary rain-cloud grey, for like the place they had come from there were no clouds. It was simply as if all the blueness had been drained from the sky – like a clear summer's day captured in an old black and white photograph. And yet, as Douglas took time to look around, it was not just the sky; from the roughly paved lane on which they were standing, across the dusty fields to the circle of houses before the hills in the distance, everything seemed to have been drained of colour. Silas's red tunic in comparison seemed almost dazzling.

It took Tom a moment longer to notice the greyness. He had been so eager to scan the landscape for the Tower, and then been disappointed not to find it. All along he had somehow *felt* it would be just beyond the Forests. Now, with no sign of it in sight, he was starting to doubt the feeling that told him the Tower was close. He was even beginning to believe that it was a trick, some of Aldred's magic – the further he travelled *away* from the Tower, the *closer* he felt it to be. It was possible.

But with nothing to prove this, and Silas and Doug looking to him for guidance, Tom climbed over the grey stone wall and started towards the houses in the distance.

"Is the Tower close now?" asked Douglas as he dropped wearily to the other side of the wall. A cloud of ash-like dust billowed up and made him splutter.

"Beyond those hills, I think."

"Fields, village, hills, Tower. We might be there before night-time," Douglas said hopefully.

The fields were divided into strips by the knee-high walls. There were no plants here, only earth a slightly darker grey than the sky. In parts it was very soft and loose and every few minutes Tom and Douglas had to stop and pour it out of their shoes. Right then both boys found themselves wishing for a sturdy pair of boots like Silas's.

About a third of the way down the field Tom's pace slowed a little.

"What is it?" asked Douglas.

Tom shrugged. He thought he had glimpsed something in the distance, some movement in the earth. But he wasn't sure. This strange greyness which covered everything like a blanket could have tricked him. Perhaps it was a shadow.

Further along the field the ground became sandier and not quite as flat. Here there were lines that curved like tiny rivers into the distance. Douglas noticed them first, but they were not, as he had first thought, ditches. They were, in fact, their opposite – *ridges* – as if there were pipes half sunk into the field, yet covered with dust so that you couldn't quite see what they were made of.

Douglas kicked one. The sand fell in. There was no pipe.

"Hollow," he murmured.

"Come on," urged Tom. "There's nothing here for us."

A sudden glumness caused Douglas to sigh.

He drew spirals in the dust with his shoe. "I thought maybe the Tower would be here," he confessed. "At least I wished it would be. But the Scroll said something about an arch, didn't it? I've not seen an arch. I've been looking hard enough."

Douglas pulled the Scroll from his pocket and carefully unrolled it. Then squinting hard at each odd word, he read:

Where it lies, no one can say
An arch, perhaps, will show the way.

He looked the question at Tom.

"Maybe," Tom suggested, "it's a bridge or ... a gateway, across the hills."

Doug shrugged absently. He was still examining the Scroll. An earlier piece had grabbed his attention.

Next, cross the flat and hueless land,
And watch for dangers in the sand.

He looked across at Tom. "What does that mean, 'dangers in the sa—'"

Something caught Doug's eye. Another ridge. It was up ahead. Up ahead where there hadn't been a ridge before. The thing that had got his attention was the fact that it was moving, moving so fast towards him that at first Douglas didn't quite know what was happening. He saw the ridge forming as it flashed his way, and he saw the huge, grey, snake-like creature burst out from the sand. He even saw its eight red eyes glowing like hot coals, but it was not until he felt the sting of it biting into his leg that he realized he was not dreaming. He remembered a sea serpent from a school story of a few terms back, and thought coldly that this was a *sand* serpent.

Doug fought to keep balance, but the serpent jerked its head and he crashed to the ground. Grit splashed his face and Douglas felt himself being dragged into the earth.

Silas ran round and began to kick at the serpent. Tom, after a stunned moment when he could do nothing but stare in horror, grabbed Doug's hand and pulled against the snake-like creature.

Douglas felt himself go back, then forward, then back again as the serpent squealed and tugged harder and wilder.

Silas kicked at the creature but his boots had worn thin and were not as tough as they looked. He dropped to his knees and began to beat the serpent with his fists.

Frantically Tom struggled like a lone tug-of-war man, but the serpent was stronger. Slowly Douglas began to break from Tom's grasp.

Soon only the creature's head was above the ground and Silas's fists seemed useless against its armour of tough scales. He needed something heavier, something harder. Something like…

He left Tom struggling and scuttled to where he had placed his drum. When he returned, the creature had sunk into the sand and was dragging Douglas inexorably down with it. Again Silas dropped to his knees and began digging into the sand, pawing like a dog until finally he uncovered the head of the serpent, and then, without another moment's delay, he raised his drum high into the air and smashed it down onto the serpent's head. Then he did it again, and again, and again.

The creature thrashed up sand but refused to release Douglas. Over the thunderous sounds of the drum you could hear its furious screams. Its very last scream was the worst of all.

The creature did not release Douglas, even when it was dead. Tom and Silas had to prise apart its jaws so that Douglas could crawl free.

"It's OK, Doug." Tom brushed sand off his brow. "It's dead."

Silas examined Douglas's bleeding leg, then tore a strip from the bottom of his shirt and bound it tightly around Doug's calf.

"Is it bad?" asked Tom, still breathless from the ordeal.

"Luckilys nothing broken."

Tom gave Douglas a relieved smile, then noticed beside him Silas's drum. The drum was smashed into small pieces that were only held together by the hide drum pad. When Silas had finished tending to Douglas he tenderly picked up the drum as if it were the body of an animal he had grown fond of, and buried it in the sand.

"Doug?" Tom touched his arm gently. "Let's see if you can stand. I don't think we should hang around here too long in case there are any more of those things around."

The thought of the serpent spurred Douglas. Clutching on to Tom's arm on one side and Silas's arm the other, he pulled himself up. He tested his leg gently, then winced as he leaned more weight on to it and hot pain shot into his knee. After a second, more cautious try, Douglas thought he could probably walk if they took it slowly.

It took them a long time to reach the end of the field but there were no more ridges in the sand and they were not bothered by any more serpents.

There was a tangle of bramble stalks running along the outside edge of the wall at the end of the field, but no fruit grew between the colourless leaves. Tom felt his stomach rumble. He looked to the curve of houses further along the lane on which they were standing and wondered if they might find food there. When the people of the village heard of their plans to finish Aldred and his terrible ways, maybe a banquet would be in order.

The village was bigger than Tom had first thought, for within the circle of houses there were other buildings. There was an inn and a shop and in the centre of the village, beside which a stream would have run had it not been dried up, there was a slightly fancier building with arched windows and a small spire. This building Tom took to be a church of some kind.

The church was quiet.

The inn was empty.

The shop was closed.

Tom was beginning to wonder if anything other than poisoned dwarfs and the mysterious sand serpent lived in this part of Edonia. Then all of a sudden the silence was broken as a door to one of the old stone houses nearby scraped open, and out stepped a short, balding man with a thick white beard and an overcoat the same shade of grey as the sky. He was calling a goodbye to somebody inside the house. In his hand he clutched a leather bag which jangled as he set off.

The boys watched as he crossed the street and entered a white stone building with a marking on the door. The mark was a cross and although the mark, like everything here, was mostly grey, Tom was sure that it had once been red.

"He's a doctor," Tom whispered. "And I bet that building's a hospital. He may have something for your leg, Doug. *He* can't be bad, can he? Not if he's a doctor."

"Dr Jekyll," Doug said crisply. "Dr Crippen! Maybe we should go to a house instead."

The first house they came to was a small whitewashed cottage with tiny windows of cloudy glass and a door made of planks held together with horseshoe nails. Upon the door was tacked a notice. Because, like the writing on the Scroll, some of the letters were capitals where there shouldn't have been capitals and some were written backwards, it was at first hard to make out the words. But after a moment they got used to the strange writing, and the notice became quite clear.

It was not what Tom had wanted to read.

The sign said:

THE NEW PRINCE IS SAVIOUR
LONG LIVE ALDRED. MASTER OF THE LIFESTREAM!

10

THE DOCTOR

The next house they came to had a similar message. Tom looked from it to the closed-up shop nearby. It too had a sign – this one was pinned to the window shutter. The boys wandered over to it.

"'Good Prince Aldred, brave and bold'?" Douglas read the first line with a frown. "I don't understand it."

With a sudden crack which startled everyone the door burst open and a large round lady, with silvery hair tied up in a bun, peered at them through a pair of tiny spectacles. "Shop's closed!" she barked. "Opens again at quittin' times."

"We're not here to buy," Tom said, surprised at the woman's gruffness. "We haven't any money."

"I makes my own brushes and boils oyster

hens a-catched from the prairie. If you're here to sells, you're a-wasting your time."

The old woman was about to say more when she noticed Douglas and eyed his clothes with suspicion. Tom searched for something to say. But then, from the corner of her eye, the woman spied something which made her forget Douglas and turn the nearest shade of red Tom had seen in this part of Edonia. She was looking at the sign on the shutter.

"Dids you do this?" she glowered at Tom.

"No. I thought you—"

Roaring, the woman ripped the sign from the shutter and frenziedly tore it into fragments no bigger than postage stamps. A moment later the boys watched the pieces flutter down the lane like odd confetti. Then all of a sudden the woman shrieked, "Damn brats!" And *slam!*

They were staring at the closed door, speechless.

They were still staring when Tom suddenly felt a cold hand on his neck. He shuddered and gasped and turned, all in an instant, and saw a figure not much bigger than himself. It was the old man they had seen earlier leaving the house across the street. He pressed his bony fingers more firmly into the flesh of Tom's neck; they tingled slightly, and in a soft, dreamlike voice the old man whispered, "You're hungry and your feet are sore."

Faster than anyone could have guessed, the man spun on his heel and reached for Douglas, again pressing his hand firmly on the side of his neck just above the shoulder. "And your leg gives great pain."

This was true. The bandage Silas had fastened around Douglas's leg had stopped the bleeding but it hadn't done much to relieve the ache.

"Yes," said Douglas.

Suddenly the man reached for Silas. He laid his fingers on Silas's neck, then snorted as he pulled his hand away and began to rub the coloured paste from his fingers.

"You," he said, "are fine. Fitter than all of us."

Five minutes later they were sitting in the cross-marked building across the street, in a white painted room with polished wooden benches against its four corners and a wall full of big old books. There was one chair in the centre of the room, a little like a barber's chair from home. The old man, Dr Beezletoff he called himself, had gone into the room next door, but an old lady in a white pinafore printed with the same grey cross as on the door, brought in a tray of bread still warm from the oven. Also on the tray were fingers of crumbly white cheese and three tankards of some liquid hidden by a thick head of froth.

The doctor returned and while Tom and Silas

ate the bread and drank the liquid (a sweet, slightly fizzy juice with a mild tanginess not unlike beer), he seated Douglas in the chair and set about tending his leg. He cut the jeans away at the knee – commenting briefly on the strangeness of the material – then bathed the cuts in a warm white liquid that smelt of aniseed. After that he smoothed the wound with paste from a large grey pot and bound it with a fresh roll of bandage. He then called on Tom to take his seat in the chair.

"This," said the doctor, "is quite an honour, young sir."

Tom did not see anything special about treating his blistered feet. "What do you mean?"

"You *are* the one from the Scroll, aren't you?"

Tom remained cautiously silent. Be wary of everything Aaron had said.

The doctor waved his question aside. "As soon as I laid my hand upon you, I knew." He dropped his voice to a whisper. "You have the *Old* Power pulsing through your veins. You have come to rid us of Aldred, yes?"

Tom looked at Douglas. He remembered all the signs in the village proclaiming Aldred's greatness.

"You," he asked cautiously, "aren't loyal to Prince Aldred?"

The old man's bitter scowl answered the

question clearly enough, but to confirm it he shook his head and cried, "That man is no prince!"

"But the writing on the houses—"

Douglas nodded. "'Good Prince Aldred, brave and bold.'"

"The young ones do it," replied the doctor. "They know no better."

Tom suddenly realized that all the people they had so far seen in the village were old.

"Where *are* the young ones?"

The doctor pointed downward. "All the children are under *his* spell, you see. He makes them dig ice-crystals from the mines beneath the prairies in return for a greater share of rations from the underground spring."

Ice-crystals, thought Tom. *They couldn't be diamonds, could they? Aldred couldn't be mining ice-crystals here to take back to the other world, where he could swap them for anything he wanted? A plane? A yacht? A fast red sports car?*

"Why," asked Silas, "do his spells not works on you?"

Douglas, feeling much better, had wandered over to the wall of books, but turned at the doctor's answer.

"We older ones know better. We remember our land before the droughts. The fields of green. The autumn festivals and the dance of the red berries."

"Did *he* make everything so grey?" asked Douglas.

"He not only drained the life from the soil, but the very colour from the sky."

"Can't you talk to the young ones? Tell them what's going on?" wondered Tom.

"It is not so easy to talk to the youngsters. They do not listen any more. The Enchantment is too strong! No, the only solution is to finish Aldred and break the spell."

"I'm looking for the Dark Tower," said Tom. "Can you show me where it is?"

A note of desperation had crept into Tom's voice.

The doctor shook his head. "I do not know where the Tower stands. I do not know anyone who does. There are some who say that the Tower no longer exists."

Tom felt his heart sink. "But we've come so far."

The old man waved him quiet. "There are others who believe the Tower exists only in the hearts of Outlanders and Descendants."

"'Follow your heart,'" whispered Tom. "That's the instruction I was given."

"And what," asked the doctor, "does your heart tell you?"

Tom sighed. "My heart says the Tower is close. But my head and my eyes and my sore feet say it could be miles away."

"If it lies northward it cannot be far away."

The three boys looked blankly at the doctor.

"See!" He strode over to the wall of books and pulled down a very large leather-backed volume. Resting it on the chair, he then opened it at its middle pages which revealed a map of the land. In the centre was the castle of Crestoban. To the left of Crestoban were the Barren Lands. To the other side of the castle was something which looked like a misshapen oval, marked as the Crystal Lake of Olam.

"Where Aldred fired the key," remembered Douglas.

"It is all but dry now," said the doctor regretfully.

"And this river –" he ran his finger along the waving line above the lake – "was once a torrent. To cross it you would have needed a good raft and a team of strong rowers."

Silas noticed a smaller river running into a patch of woodland in the bottom right-hand corner of the map.

"That's Tall Trees!" He nodded excitedly. "That's my home. Tallest trees in the land."

Douglas looked at him in surprise. "Taller even that the Pitch Forests?"

"Two or threes as tall, easy."

"You hear that, Tom?"

Tom *hadn't* heard. He had just realized what the doctor had meant when he said that if the Tower lay further north, then it must be close. Because he saw their current position on the map – beyond the Pitch Forests (which stretched like a thin dark band almost right across the country) but before the faint line of the Whispering Hills. Beyond the hills was a small, featureless strip marked as the Waste of Rynn, and after that an area of uniform waving lines which was, Tom realized, because he had seen old maps in encyclopedias and storybooks, the sea.

"How far are the hills?" asked Tom.

"Two or three candlespans."

Tom looked blankly at the doctor, who had folded the book closed and was replacing it.

"He means theys not far." Silas grinned. "These northerns-folk people talks a bit oddlys. If we go quick we shoulds be there soon."

"Then I think we should hurry," urged Tom with no real reason except for a strange feeling in his heart – an odd notion that he was being followed. He tried to tell himself that things were too important now to spoil everything by rushing ahead like a silly schoolboy on a childish dare.

But it did not work. The feeling did not go. So bidding the doctor thanks and farewell, they set off once more for the Whispering Hills.

Many miles east of the Whispering Hills, just beyond the deserted military camp of Askrigg

Hill, where the trees of the Pitch Forest were stopped from plummeting over the sea-thrashed cliffs only by a thin band of stone, the sound of a horn cut through the air. A sea bird, something like an enormous black gull which had been spiralling overhead, darted into the cover of the trees. Drawing his stallion to a halt, Aldred peered into the Forest. His five followers stopped and stared too.

The pale-faced creature that appeared stayed well within the shadows.

"Closer," commanded Aldred, "so that I can see you."

The creature shuffled nervously, then moved only a little way forward.

"The boy," said Aldred, sensing its discomfort. "You *have* brought the boy with you?"

The white face drew further back, then in a voice which trembled with fear, the creature cried, "The Outlander has, my great Lord, es ... escaped us."

Aldred sat up so fast his stallion almost bolted.

"Escaped!"

Spit sprayed from Aldred's mouth. His fingers clenched and twitched violently. From the index finger of his right hand there shot splinters of purple light which hit the ground and left patches of smouldering earth.

"How could he have escaped?"

The reply was timid and mouselike. "There

are three of them. Two Outlanders and a drummer boy from the Tall Trees. He tricked us with thunderberries."

Aldred's eyes turned a fierce red.

"I think," gasped the creature in the trees, "I think one of the boys has some of the old magic. He—"

The creature uttered not one more word. Aldred blinked and turned the creature and the trees around it into a giant field of flame.

"Three," murmured Aldred. "But only one may enter the Tower."

The heat from the spreading flames was becoming fierce. Aldred backed his horse away and turned to the knights behind him.

"Return to Crestoban and await instruction. If news gets out about this there may be a rebellion. I shall go on and put an end to the Summerville brat myself."

The hills had been further than Tom had expected. He should have guessed that *his* idea of "Not far" would be quite different from Silas's "Not fars". But after several hours' walking, with a break to kick grit from their shoes, then another to eat waxy chunks of pale chocolate-like sweets that the doctor had given them, they reached their goal.

On setting out, Silas had said that they could reach the hills well before nightfall. Had they kept Silas's naturally fast pace, this might have been true. As it was, with aching feet and tired hearts, they reached the foot of the hills just as night was sweeping over them. The air here felt different, thought Tom. It was still hot, still dry. But now it *smelt* dry too; electrical, as if a monster of a storm were brewing.

"The Dark Tower," Tom whispered without knowing it. He was glancing up at the shadowy hills. The pictures its name conjured in his mind had always been worrying. But now, at nightfall, they took on a more sinister edge. Tom had read enough stories to know such badness; bad things and bad places begin to stir as darkness falls. When the sun goes down, something deeper, something darker seems to awaken. At least that's the way it was with every playground ghost tale he had ever heard. Soon it would be midnight. The witching hour.

Tom sank to the ground, slipped off his shoe and sock and cautiously probed the sole of his foot. The skin was red and becoming sore again.

"I think we ought to rest here. At least until the sun comes up," he suggested. Although up in the hills not so much as a mouse stirred, Tom dared not raise his voice above a whisper.

Douglas nodded agreement.

"This is a good place to camp," said Silas.

They talked until it was fully dark, then one by one they drifed into sleep. Douglas first, then Silas. Tom stayed awake a while longer, holding the key in his hands but seeing nothing more than a shadow. A vague shadow that was part of a vague task to rescue a forgotten prince.

Tom finally drifted off just as the hills began whispering.

In Douglas's dream they whispered a tale of Tom and Silas ditching him in the desert with no food and no water and no map to find his way out. In Silas's mind the hills whispered a cry of betrayal from his Tall Trees homeland. Tom tossed and turned with a dream of Greenvale and the day of the boating accident. The hills said, *It's your fault, Tom. You coward. Your fault.*

Dust billowed up as he thrashed around. Tears squeezed out of the corner of his eyes.

Your fault. You coward. Your fault. You coward. Your fault.

No!

He sat up. It was daylight. The sun beat down on his neck with the hotness of an angry slap. Turning his head slightly he squinted up at the hills. Even in daylight they appeared dark and cold. But then he noticed something above them. Something which made him wonder for a moment if he were not still dreaming. Beside him Doug and Silas were sleeping. The jacket Douglas had used to cover himself in the night had slid down to his waist. Tom gently pulled it back up to shade his neck from the sun. Then he looked up at the hills again, and it was still there – a rainbow. It was like a rainbow back home except that this rainbow had no colour to it – just different shaded bands of grey, from the lightest shade of a wagtail's egg to the inner band that was almost black.

Tom felt for the key, then realized that he had fallen asleep with it in his hand. Now it lay half buried in the dust near where he had stirred awake. Tom spotted it easily, but next to it there was something he hadn't noticed quite so quickly – a message. Six simple words cut into the dust as if someone had scrawled them there with the tip of a shaky index finger.

Six simple words. One simple sentence.

Go on and you will die.

Tom scrambled to his feet and backed quickly away as if from a poisonous snake. He blinked. Far away a model Chieftain tank swung its gun forward. Tom blinked again. Looked closer.

The words were gone.

Tom's movements had woken Silas. Tom nudged Douglas awake. "Look, Doug." He pointed up at the rainbow, but it was already fading. The darkest band that had earlier seemed almost black was only a dull grey now. "It's the arch. *'An arch, perhaps, will show the way.'*"

Douglas's sleepiness left him immediately as a sudden relief rushed over him and he began to laugh.

Silas found the arch puzzling. "What is it?" he asked warily. "Some of Aldred's magic?"

"No. It's a rainbow," said Tom. "I think there's a storm coming."

11

THE GUARDIAN

"Listen," said Tom. "When we reach the Tower, I have to go on alone. Remember what the Scroll said: 'Only one can enter there'."

It was some time since the sinister message had blown away, and they had almost reached the top of the hills. Only the darkest band of the rainbow remained. Faint though it was, this sign of hope made the climb easier for everyone.

Douglas had pulled the Scroll from his pocket once again, pleased that at last they had a sign that they were close now.

Then travel fast and travel light
On to the place where day meets night
Where it lies no one can say
An arch perhaps will show the way
Climb the steps as fast you can
But beware the evil –

"Beware the evil *what*?"

Tom shrugged. *He* had been thinking of the earlier line:

On to the tower where day *meets* night?

Silas looked down at the Scroll and pointed to the last line.

"It all rhymes. That missing word musts rhyme with the last word of the line befores."

At the top the hills levelled off before falling gently down to a plain of what looked like heather. Beyond it you could see a thin grey band of sea. No buildings obstructed the view.

Tom stopped. He tried to speak, but something caught in his throat and nothing came out. Silas stared out at the sea. Doug looked at Tom. A puzzled frown had twisted his face into an angry knot.

"Tom?"

"It should be here," Tom said weakly. "The Tower should be right here."

Doug kicked at the dirt.

"Perhaps, further along the hills," suggested Silas with no real hope in his voice.

Suddenly Tom felt angry with himself. Angry and foolish.

"What?" he cried. "Another ten miles. Twenty. Another hundred Edonian fieldspans? No. I was wrong. It should be here and it's not." Tom began to pace along the flat ridge of the hilltop.

"'Follow your heart,'" he said. Tom stopped to spit out a bitter little laugh. "And I believed him. I must have been crazier than he was."

Silas sank glumly to the ground next to where Douglas had lowered himself. Before them Tom paced back and forth like a mechanical toy. Ten paces, then turning, all the time wringing his hands, kicking up clouds of dust with each angry turn. "That crazy old bat had enough screws loose to sink a battleship and I believed him."

Douglas brushed sweat-damped hair from his eyes and rested his head on his palms. He looked at Silas, whose hands were nervously drumming on his knee. Both wished for something to say. Neither found it. Tom was rambling now. His angry steps carrying him faster and longer.

"Keep away from the edge, Tom!" Doug called. "Watch where you're going."

"Oh, I was wrong, Doug. I was wrong about Aaron and wrong about the Tower. And maybe I'm wrong about Prince Tyso too. Maybe I can't save him. Maybe he's already dead."

Tom was sweating now, and his breathing was quick and shallow – like someone startled out of a nightmare. His pacing had become faster. So fast that what happened next took only an instant. Just the time needed to take one quick step.

One step it was daytime.

The next it was night.

In less than the time it took Tom's heart to beat just once, everything had changed. The air was no longer hot and dry. It was cold and dark, and a heavy mist swirled in a chilly wind that was almost gusting.

Several hundred yards away was a dark rise of cliff, shimmering with the dampness the mist created, and at the top of the cliff stood a building. A tall, dark building perched like a castle of a storybook kingdom of long ago. But it was not a castle. It was a church. All Hallows Church at Greenvale.

"No!" Tom shook his head and blinked.

The Dark Tower!

Aware of the cold now through his thin peasant's shirt, smelling the salt dampness on the wind, he looked again and realized.

The church.

The Tower.

The etching on the watch.

All three. The same.

Yes, it was the church of home. But on that cliff it seemed taller and darker and strangely misshapen, as if some unnatural wind had blown it all long and twisted.

So, yes it was the church. And the church was the Tower.

At a distance the cliff had looked sheer and

unclimbable, but it was, Tom found on closer inspection, formed of a slate-like rock marred with pits and shelves that made climbing – if not easy – possible. But he had to be careful. The surface was made slippery by the mist and in certain places it was soft and crumbling. Here and there feathery vines hung down invitingly, but Tom felt sure that were he to venture too close to one it would clasp his neck the way some of the Forest plants had earlier lashed at his ankles.

Back home Tom was a good climber. He could scale the tallest tree in Thorpe Wood and this rock climbing was pretty much the same: Stretching out as far as possible, feeling blindly with hands, feet, knees, elbows which bump or ledge was strongest – most trustworthy. *Yes*, thought Tom. *Not much different from the trees back home.* Except that all the trees Tom had ever scaled back home had been lit by helpful sunlight, with never more than a mild breeze to sway his balance. Oh yes, and not even the tallest larch in Thorpe Wood was one quarter the height of this cliff. At about the height of the tallest tree in Thorpe Wood, Tom found a narrow ledge and allowed himself a moment to catch his breath. He thought about Doug and Silas and hoped they were OK.

Another strong gust brought a wave of mist as thick and salty as a breaker of sea spray. Tom dug his fingers deeper into the rock and waited for the wind to ease before continuing. At about three times the height of the tallest tree in Thorpe Wood Tom reached out his left foot, pushed himself higher and without warning the slate beneath his shoe crumbled. And like the broken pieces of falling stone, Tom dropped too. His fingers clawed at the rock, but it broke away like wet plaster. Slivers of slate cut under his fingernails and showered chippings over his face. He was sure he would die. *Dead* was the one word in his mind as his feet hit a ledge barely three inches deep and he stopped sliding. Like waking from a nightmare, it was some time before he could do anything but shake. Then a shadow rose up, a heavy black shape that flapped towards him. It was a bird. Something like a raven only bigger. Its wide-open beak seemed too long and sharp pointed, its mouth too big. As it flapped its huge black wings it let out a screech so dreadful that Tom almost released his clutch on the rock just to cover his ears. Instead he screeched back, "Go away. Go away, bird. *Leave me alone!*"

In response the bird fluttered back, tilted its head to the sky and ... *laughed*. Half cackle, half caw. As it rose up and away, turning bigger and bigger circles, Tom could hear it laughing and cawing.

"Go on and die, Tom. Go on and die..."

The bird lost itself in the blackness above

the ledge and its crazed calling followed it. Tom began climbing again.

He was close to the top now. One good surge, he told himself, and he would make it. When he looked up this positive thought went in a terrified gasp.

Sometimes you see something out of the corner of your eye, a dark sinister shape as real as the shock that jolts your heart, until you realize the thing that had been studying you with its slyly watchful eyes was nothing more than a shadow among shadows.

Now Tom saw it, at the top of the cliff – a twisted half skeleton, half monster with yellow cat's eyes and same coloured teeth as long and pointed as those of a wild dog's. And with the next swirl of mist, it was gone.

Just a shadow among shadows.

Tom tried to laugh but the laugh didn't come. Grimly he moved further up the cliff. Two more climbs and he could almost reach his hand over the edge. One more, at about the height of the tallest building in Tom's town back home, and the narrow ledge of rock on which Tom was perched crumbled. Tom clung to the cliff by his fingers alone. Hot fear jumped to his throat. Cramping pain burned into his hands. His feet scrambled for purchase but found nothing. The rock was smoother here, there was not even a vine to grasp in desperation.

Absurdly, Tom cried for help.

Crazily he heard a reply.

"Here, Tom. Here."

From the corner of his mind the thing on the cliff top was back, looking down, watching. For a moment Tom saw it staring, then fade into the shadows. Hanging tightly with his right hand Tom flung his left hand up and finally found the cliff top. With aching effort he pulled himself higher until his right foot discovered a small nub of rock strong enough to support him. One quick push now and he would be able to—

"Here, Tom..."

A hand seized his wrist.

Terror seized his throat.

But it was not the skeleton creature Tom thought he had glimpsed which pulled him to safety. It was a young man. A young man with soft blue eyes and a serene smile. The flowing white robe he wore made him look somehow holy. His voice was smooth and warm.

"Thank the stars you are safe."

"Yes," replied Tom without thinking. Now he had time to look at the man more closely he realized that the reason he appeared holy to him was because he looked like a painting of Peter the Apostle which hung above the blackboard in the school's R.E. room.

After a moment Tom turned his gaze across the shadowy patch of shrubland to where the

Tower waited. Here, shining in the dampness, the building looked as long and twisted and ugly as the monster he thought he had seen on the cliff edge.

"Did you bring the key?" asked the young man softly. "You *did* bring it, didn't you?"

Suddenly cautious, Tom turned. "Who are you?"

"You were not told about me?"

Tom shook his head unsurely. Over the last week he had been told so much, maybe he had missed it in the confusion.

"I am the guardian of the Tower." The young man reached out his hand in greeting. Automatically Tom took a wary step backwards, and the guardian smiled, an easy smile. He lowered the hand with a trace of a laugh and in a voice as smooth and even as a slow-running stream, whispered, "Come now. We must hurry. The prince awaits us."

Entering the Tower was far easier than Tom had dared to imagine. The guardian (whose name, Tom learnt as they crossed the damp wasteland together, was Marius) simply pushed a palm on the big arched door and in it swung with a long, low screech worthy of all the best horror films. Instantly a terrible stench, a thick mix of melting wax, damp mould and rotten meat billowed out.

Tom had to alter his breathing so he could

take the air in through his mouth and avoid the smell.

Marius moved into the main hall of the Tower. As Tom followed he saw that he was standing in the nave of the old church at home – All Hallows, lit by the smoky flicker of candles mounted in tall, black metal sconces. In the dull light Tom could discern the soft outlines of long wooden benches, pews and the centre isle which separated them. Just like the church he remembered – except that it was bigger and not quite the straight rectangle he remembered. Here it seemed oddly out of shape, although Tom could not tell whether it was the floor that slanted or the walls that leaned, or the ceiling that sloped. Maybe, he thought, it was all three. As his eyes adjusted to the strange light Tom noticed another difference. The walls of this church were not decorated with old brasses and ornamental crosses, but with swords and rifles – above the altar two large swords crossed each other like the crossbones on a pirate flag. Tom's gaze moved along and there in the corner, beneath a dark, stained-glass window in which a knight was rising from the waves of a purple sea, was the start of the stairway. It was the stairway which led up to the spire, Tom knew from the old church back home. Pulling the key from the pouch and clutching it tightly, Tom started for it.

But he only *started* for it; for the guardian, with a distinct lack of the grace he had earlier shown, reached for Tom and pulled him back. The move had been so sudden that Tom almost tumbled.

"Not there," gasped Marius. "Danger lies that way. You must follow me. Follow the guardian, do you understand?"

Tom understood the fright in Marius's voice. He understood the word danger and nodded. Soon after Tom was following the guardian *down* the spiral stairway which began in the opposite corner of the church, close to the doorway through which they had entered. Back home the stairway led down to All Hallows crypt, but here, Tom figured, it probably ran on to a dungeon of some kind. With only one candle, hastily plucked by Marius from a holder, it was rather gloomy but Tom still noticed that although the candle was white, the drips that splashed on to the stone steps were as deep a red as any man's blood. But this may have been the shadows playing tricks. In this watery light the guardian's gown seemed darker, duller and here and there mottled with cloudy patches of damp or mould.

Down they travelled, past the point at which the All Hallows crypt should have been and on into darkness and the kettledrum pounding of Tom's heart. Tom didn't like it on the stairway.

The steps sloped in such an odd way it was hard to walk. It was too dark. Too narrow. The dank smells of mould and bad meat were stronger down here and that flickering light continued to play tricks; for the guardian's gown looked like coarse grey sack cloth now, and his flowing hair had lost its sheen. Tom even thought he could see bare patches shining through.

"Come, boy, quickly." The guardian gasped without looking back. At his waist, tucked into a frayed rope belt which Tom had not noticed before, was a yellow metal cross. Not a golden yellow, but dull yellow, like the teeth of the monster on the cliff.

"Just a trick of the light," Tom told himself, and on they travelled. Down and down.

"Are we close now?" asked Tom in a nervous whisper.

The guardian's reply was far less reserved. It was a quick, shrill laugh which almost snuffed the only source of light they had. Tom shivered. "It's so dark in here."

"Always dark in the Dark Tower, Tom." The guardian replied in a voice which sounded higher, less smooth than it had before. Then he gave out another short laugh, more of a cackle this time, as his free hand traced over the cross at his belt. The cross was long and sharp pointed – like the guardian's fingernails. Strange, Tom hadn't noticed his nails before.

And on they went. Tom following the guardian instead of following his heart as he had been told to do. His heart had said, *Up in the spire*. But here he was, going in the opposite direction. And now his heart was whispering, *Something's wrong. Get out of here, now.*

"You *do* have the key, don't you, Tom?"

The guardian had turned to face Tom but continued leading him down, walking backwards down the awkwardly sloping steps as easily as he walked forward, his dull grey eyes studying the hand in which Tom tightly clutched the key. He licked his lips.

"You have brought my key, haven't you?"

A sudden thought hit Tom like a slap across his face.

Blue. His eyes were blue.

"Where's my key?"

Blue. Clear blue, like the eyes of the painting at school.

Tom stopped.

The guardian ceased his downward slide.

"Come, Tom. Time's-a-wasting."

"You know my name," said Tom as he searched his mind for a simple explanation for these changes – the light? Or himself, seeing things that aren't really there – jumping at shadows, as his mother used to say? In his head the voice of reason whispered, *Calm down, Tom. The man is here to help.*

158

In his chest, his pounding heart admitted a growing doubt.

Doubts were troubling Douglas too. He had pulled the Scroll from his pocket, and as the blazing Edonian sun burned his neck and lit the Scroll much lighter than the dull yellow it actually was, he ran the last two lines of it over and over in his head.

Climb the stairs as fast as you can
But beware the evil...

What?

Seated cross-legged beside him, Silas was diligently rubbing dirt from his tunic the way a person might hand wash a favourite shirt. Dust sprinkled, like dark icing sugar, to the ground and the colour returned to the cloth like magic. The tunic again reminded Douglas of some old-fashioned military uniform.

Silas caught Douglas's gaze. "Must look goods for the Resistance. They choose only the best. Good fighters. Smartest and the bests."

"If only we could find them," Douglas whispered to himself.

As if he had heard, Silas said, "I heards from a clovecaster gypsy that they was up here in the Northern lands."

Douglas looked at the silver grey line of sea that divided the land from the sky not far to his right. They could hardly go further north, he realized, and he knew then that Silas's heroes were not going to ride up like the cavalry from an old Western movie and save the day. He dropped his gaze sadly to his feet and heaved out a long sigh.

He checked himself in mid-breath and threw his head up again. Something, just a fragment of darkness against the brightness that surrounded them, had caught his eye. It was ... he blinked, not sure if it was there any more – if it had been there at all. But yes, it had simply disappeared into a dip in the hills.

"Look!" Doug called and pointed. "What is it, Silas?"

To Douglas it appeared to be little more than a dark speck, like a tiny sunspot with no real shape. He guessed that it was moving, but behind a curtain of rippling heatwaves, he could not tell if it were heading towards or away from them.

Silas's eyes seemed able to cut through the haze. After a short time squinting out across the crest of the hills, he said, "It's a rider ... coming this way." After another pause he added, "Wearing black. Coming fasts."

Douglas capped his hands above his eyes. Now that it was closer he could make out the basic shape. But beyond this he could tell nothing. To Douglas it looked like a lone black chess piece on a board way across a room. Yet a wild kind of hope began to stir in him. "He may know the Resistance, Silas. He may even be one of them!"

Silas remained silent. Slowly the light and dark lines across his brow began to ripple into a curious frown. The horse seemed to be galloping faster than Silas had ever imagined a horse possibly could. In fact, it appeared as if the hoofs of the animal were not touching the ground at all, but riding a path of air just above it.

Douglas jumped to his feet. "If he's one of the Resistance, maybe he'll help us." Now Douglas could see what Silas had earlier described – a horse and rider, approaching at a gallop. In his mind's eye Douglas saw a bold knight, weary from battle but ready to fight again in his valiant struggle against the evil prince. Silas, close beside Douglas yet seeing far clearer, saw something else – something worse. Much worse.

12

ALDRED AND THE PRINCE

"I know a lot about you, Tom," whispered the guardian as they continued down the cold stone stairway. "I am the guardian. It's my duty. Now, the key. Give it to me."

The guardian looked from Tom's tightly clenched hand, in which he held the key, to Tom himself, and suddenly Tom's legs turned to water. The guardian's eyes, which had turned from blue in the hall to a dull watery grey down here in the lone candle dimness, were now neither blue nor grey. They were ...

(Tom tried to swallow, but his mouth had dried as it had in the Forest.)

... *yellow*. His eyes were yellow. With tall, black, cat-like centres. His teeth had changed too. Now they were like the cross at his waist, long, yellow and sharp. Behind its curled upper lip Tom could see its black gums, shiny with spittle.

Sometimes you see something out of the corner of your eye. Most times it's just a shadow among shadows. Most times...

Tom screamed, turned, ran. An ancient hand clamped around his ankle and he hit the steps as if he had dived badly into a swimming pool, knocking the wind from his chest and the sense from his head. And like a poor swimmer in that pool Tom began to claw and kick wildly, and somehow in the panic he began to pull against the hand.

"My key, Tom. Where's my key?"

Like everything about the thing that had once seemed saintly, its voice had become terribly twisted – like the gargling shriek of something drowning. Tom kicked more wildly and clawed at the steps until his nails broke and his fingers burned, and finally his foot broke free. He scrambled fast, slipped, tried once more and moved just one step when the cross, actually a sharp pointed dagger, came whistling down. It made a sickening, tearing sound as it ripped though Tom's shirt, a noise quite out of proportion to the action which created it. In here that simple *rrrriipppp* seemed almost deafening.

Tom looked back, saw the damage and almost fainted. He saw blood where the knife had pinned his shirt to the crumbling stone. But the blade, he realized, had not cut deep into his skin. Not much more than a graze. The relief was dizzying. *Thank goodness,* Tom thought crazily, *for this baggy old shirt.* And he laughed at the stupidity of it. Suddenly, as if troubled by his laughter, the guardian-thing faltered. It released its clutch on the knife and drew away. Without stopping to think, Tom reached for the blade and pulled it from the stone. It felt icy cold in his hand and blood dripped from its point like the wax from the candle, which lay still burning several steps below.

Tom wanted to run, but he fought the urge and climbed slowly to his feet. Like a symbol of triumph he held the cross erect before him and cried, "*I* am the guardian now!"

The creature with yellow eyes cowered into the shadows.

"The Tower is mine. *Go now!*"

The horror shrank down and away. Tom wedged the cross into his belt and picked up the fallen candle. Then, following his heart, he started *upward.*

Before the rider got much closer Douglas had realized that he was not one of the Resistance, although he wasn't sure why. Perhaps it was the way Silas, beside him, seemed to tense as the figure came into view. Maybe it was the way the black-clad rider was callously whipping the panting horse, as no good man would.

Or was it that Douglas saw something in that dark outline which reminded him of the shadowy figure shooting fire from its fingers, that night in the lane?

Whichever the reason, Douglas recognized even from a distance that there was no good to this man. No good at all.

The distance between the rider and the boys was shrinking fast. Even Douglas could see details now. Behind the man his black cape flapped wildly like a witch's cloak.

Silas's hand gripped Douglas's arm. "It's him!" he cried. "It's Prince Aldred. The evil one!"

Douglas froze. He dared not look at Silas or even blink. With every second the rider got closer and closer until Douglas could see the horse's hoofs were not touching the ground. They kicked up no dust and made no sound. All Douglas heard was the panting of the horse and the crack of the whip.

The horse was close now. Close and getting closer.

Fifteen yards. Thirteen. Eleven. Nine.

It came so fast that Doug had little time to ponder the damage the rampaging horse might do to his flesh and bone. He briefly remembered a boy at school who was once kicked by a small seaside pony and now walked with a permanent limp. Douglas pictured a small pony and then tried to compare it to this horse.

But before Douglas could think, the stallion leapt into the air. Purple light flashed around it and a deafening thunderclap shook the ground. By the time the rumble faded, the horse and its rider were gone.

Tom stepped into the candle-lit hall, shaking. Crossing it diagonally from one stairway to the other, he tried not to look too closely at the shadows. They seemed to be moving.

In the same dark and narrow way that the first stairway had spiralled down, this one twisted upward. Tom lost no time in climbing the stairway, and soon he found himself on a landing on which there were two doors facing each other. One was lit by a single candle. The other was drenched in the glow from many candles set in a beautiful golden sconce.

Both doors had keyholes large enough to take the key. The hole to the bright door was edged in polished brass. The hole on the smaller, darker door was encrusted with rust. Across the peeling surface of the dark door someone had brushed a thick red cross – the kind of mark, Tom recalled from school, that was once splashed across the door of a house fallen foul of the plague. The other door was painted bright yellow with red edging, and seeping from beneath it was a smell of candy-floss and hot dogs. A foul animal stench oozed out from the door marked with the cross.

Tom turned the key over in his hand and started for the bright door. But before he reached it, he stopped, looked back and forth from door to door as Aaron's shaky voice drawled in his head: "Be wary of *everything*." Tom suddenly wondered if it could be a trap. The sweet smells luring him in. But then, he looked back at the peeling door and thought, *Maybe I'm supposed to think it's a trap and go back to the door, which is the real trap.*

Somewhere below, Tom thought he heard the sound of galloping hooves, but then they were gone. More tricks. He shrugged and slotted the key into the shiny brass keyhole and turned it.

The lock clicked smoothly. Tom pressed his hand on the door and gently pushed. Immediately the smell of the fairground was replaced by a musty smell which reminded Tom of a dusty, old-fashioned bookshop back home. His mum's favourite shop.

Tom took a cautious step forward. The room which revealed itself was not the prison cell Tom had been expecting. No rats scurried across the floor and there were no chains hanging from damp, grey stone walls. The walls *were* grey stone, but they were neither damp nor bare. Hung across them were paintings and tapestries. In the thin light trickling in from one tall, arched window, Tom could just make out that they were mostly of great battles between armies of armoured horsemen.

His footsteps dulled as he stepped in and, looking down, Tom saw that the floor was spread with a rich red carpet. A cluster of model soldiers, armoured knights, some on horseback, were grouped upon the carpet in a complex battle formation. Tom noticed that one of the models looked similar to his old clockwork jouster. There was a lot of furniture in the room: two buttoned leather chairs, one long oak table and a smaller, darker table on which a burned out candle and a bowl of dead flowers stood. The chairs, the tables and even the flowers were softened by a thin veil of cobwebs, and it was because of this that Tom did not at first notice the largest object in the room. It was a bed – one with a tall post at each corner. The cobwebs covered the bed from post to post, and when Tom finally did notice it he thought somebody had spread a lace sheet over it.

At first the cobwebs worried Tom, but then he thought back to the spiders in the Forest and wondered if an ordinary sized spider would ever upset him again.

Movement turned his thoughts away from spiders. Tom looked at the bed. The shadow of a hand appeared behind the cobweb. It hung in the air a moment, then began to claw at the web. From the bed came a sound, something like a groan, and Tom stepped back. A cold feeling began to crawl over him. It reminded him of the night in the lane back home when he had first encountered Aldred. There was a strange electrical smell in the air. A feeling that Aldred was close sent a shiver down his spine.

He turned, knocking over a half-filled metal tankard and several of the mounted soldiers, and over the quiet commotion there was another sound.

"Wait!"

It was a strange voice. Except, Tom realized as he reached the doorway, that it was not really strange. It was simply not what he had expected to hear in a place such as the Dark Tower. It was too soft and pleasant. It was the voice of a child.

Tom turned. There was a boy on the bed. A boy of about Tom's age, or perhaps a year older. He sat up, peeled away the cobweb and then stretched as if just wakened from a long sleep. He was wearing a blue, knee-length tunic belted at the waist and edged with golden braid. His hair was shoulder-length and golden and across his forehead ran a thin band of golden metal.

He was squinting at Tom.

"Who are you? What are you doing here?"

The feeling that Aldred was close swept away Tom's caution.

"I'm looking for the prince," he said quickly. "Prince Tyso. I don't think I have much time."

The boy yawned and rubbed his eyes. "I must have fallen asleep. I think my cousin dropped slumber berries into the water I drank last night."

Shakily the boy got to his feet. When he began to sway and it looked as if he might suddenly fall back, Tom rushed to steady him.

"Thank you ... friend."

"My name is Tom," replied Tom, hurriedly.

"And mine," the boy broke to stifle a yawn, "is Tyso."

Tom froze. The boy was glancing around the room. He ran a hand over the small table beside his bed and seemed surprised to see dust running through his fingers.

Tom stepped closer. "*Prince* Tyso?"

The boy nodded.

"I thought you'd be ... older," said Tom. Then he remembered the story of Sleeping Beauty, who did not age during her long slumber. A noise from below distracted Tom. It was a click. Perhaps a door opening or closing...

The boy snapped upright. "It's my cousin!" he cried, reaching for the sword and scabbard which rested on the table. "He has returned. Aldred and his men dragged me from my castle at Crestoban last night and locked me in here."

"Not last night," Tom explained as he urged the prince to hurry down the twisting stairway. "You were taken from the castle many years ago. I think you have been asleep for a long time. It was only when I opened the door that you woke. A lot of bad things have happened in Edonia since you have been ... away."

Startled by this news, the prince slowed his pace. Tom grabbed his hand and pulled him on.

As they wound their way down the stairway Tom briefly told what he knew. He mentioned the droughts and the bad crops, the children working as slaves under the Greyland Prairies and Aldred's army of freed criminals – the Knights of the New Order.

He finished as they reached the bottom of the stairway.

There was something different about the hall, thought Tom, although what the change was he could not say. The candles, though they had burned lower, still flickered and the smell of hot wax and smoke was as strong as ever, but underneath it was another smell – the smell of a storm brewing.

Tyso gripped Tom's arm tightly. "He's here, I can feel it."

Tom peered into the corners where it was darkest, but it was the wall above the altar that drew his attention. Where earlier two large swords had crossed, there now hung only one.

Behind the boys the missing sword glinted yellow in the candlelight. The low swiping sound it made as it cut through the air made them both turn fast. At first all Tom saw was the gleaming blade; the man in black who held it blended so well into the shadows it seemed as if he belonged with them.

But then both boys noticed his eyes. Behind the sword Aldred's eyes burned like hot coals. Although the hall was not so cold, each breath he gave out turned white in the air. Tom noticed that he was looking at him, not the prince.

"I gave you the chance to turn back and you refused it. Never again will you be so foolish."

Aldred gripped the sword so tightly that Tom heard every bone in his hand crack. Tom saw the sword-arm rise to its full height, and in that instant he thought of home and Aunt Jess and school and Douglas – but mostly he thought about dying.

Tom closed his eyes. A second later he felt pain cut into his shoulder. But it was not the sword. The prince, with all his speed and might, had pulled Tom away. As the blade swiped the air where Tom had stood, Tom slammed into the altar steps. Pain, something like sinking into too hot bath water, spread over his back. Water welled in his eyes and for a moment he could see nothing but greyness. But he could still hear.

He heard the young prince draw his sword and start forward.

"Your quarrel is with me and my people, Aldred. Not with the Outlander boy. Now I give you the chance to turn back."

Aldred threw back his head and barked out a chilling laugh. When he looked at the prince his eyes blazed redder than before and his upper lip was curled like a wild dog's.

"Prepare," he grinned, "to die."

The first clash of metal brought an explosion of sparks. Then again and again as Aldred swiped and the prince, groggy and dazed from his long sleep, managed to counter the blows, flashes of brilliant light cracked from the blades like lightning.

Tom looked to the sword above the altar and wondered if he might tackle Aldred with one good thrust. His back ached badly and his right arm had twisted in the fall, and even if he hadn't fallen, the speed and passion with which Tyso and Aldred were fighting made him doubt if he could even get close. Both appeared to be expert swordsmen, and the fight seemed obviously one to the death. But he had to do something. With pain cutting into his shoulder like a lance, Tom reached for the sword, but with one quick glance from Aldred it was enveloped in purple sparks. A moment later it dripped like melted plastic into a glowing pool on the stone in front of Tom. Some of it splashed onto his shoe and it began to smoulder. In front of him the blades clashed again.

Aldred was nimble for such a large man, and

for a boy thrust suddenly into the fight, the prince was quick, though his actions were governed by instinct and training rather than true alertness. And instinct alone is not enough to keep a heavy sword raised when muscles not used in years begin to weaken. This time, when Aldred thrust, the prince was not fast enough. His robe reddened at the shoulder, where the blade had cut. The prince looked at the wound and wavered momentarily and with an animal grunt, Aldred raised the sword above his head and swung again. Just in time Tyso lifted his sword, but his grip had weakened and the sword was sent flying from his hand. It clattered across the floor, pushing over several of the candle holders. Some of the spilled candles, Tom saw, rolled to one of the dry wooden benches which began to smoulder and then flame. When Tom looked back to the fight Aldred was standing over the fallen prince, his own sword raised high for the killing blow.

Many thoughts flooded into Tom's mind right then. Thoughts of the long journey that had brought him here and the terrible thought that he had done it all just to see the prince killed. He recalled the watch and the Forest people and the spiders. And then he remembered the biggest spider and how he had killed it. Forgetting his aching back and his twisted arm, he sprang to his feet and whipped the gun from his pants.

"STOP!" The gunsight held Aldred dead centre. It was not loaded, Tom realized, but he remembered the ball of fire that had killed the spider and was sure that the same would happen again. It was the power of the Old Kings.

"Drop your sword!" Tom cried. To his surprise his voice did not shake. "Drop it or I shall fire."

"No, Tom!" gasped the prince. "You must not use the Old Power here."

"Yes," whispered Aldred, so softly Tom didn't hear him.

Behind him the burning bench began to crackle and spit.

"Shoot me now, if you have the courage," said Aldred. "I don't think you dare. It takes a lot to kill a man."

"You're not a man," spat Tom.

"Then you have nothing to fear. You have a choice, Tom. It's time for you to choose. Light or dark? Am I to run your friend through this very minute or are you to save him?"

On the ground the prince tried to turn, but Aldred raised his foot and pressed a heavy boot on his neck.

It made it difficult for Tyso to speak.

"Itsh-a-tri... Tohhhmmmm. Dohhhhnnnn..."

The flames from the first burning bench had caught the second bench and over the crackling it was hard for Tom to hear.

"Mussnn use the ol' ower ... ainst others who ... oh it... Soak it uhhh. Becommm ... onger."

Aldred's voice rose above the flames. "I brought you here, Tom, because I need your help. The Power has changed me – turned me bad. I need to find peace. Only you can save me."

The prince tried shifting his position. "Dohhnn ... isten, Tom. Heeeesh ... ying." Tom did not see Aldred move, but his boot pressed harder onto Tyso's neck. Tyso was finding it difficult to breathe.

The anger had gone from Aldred's eyes. Or perhaps the smoke that had begun to fold down from the ceiling in layers simply dulled them. "I murdered your parents, Tom. You must avenge them. For *them*, for *Edonia* and for *yourself*, pull the trigger."

All Tom caught over the crackle and hiss of the burning benches were the words *killed* and *parents*. He heard nothing of the prince's calls. His hand gripped the gun tightly, his finger curled around the trigger and without hesitation he fired, not once, not twice, but three times. And each time he squeezed the trigger a bolt of light more brilliant than lightning flashed from the barrel. At once the high beams running across the roof burst into flames. As they burned something strange happened – although Tom shot the deadly bolts surely into the air, Aldred dropped to his knees as if all three had hit him.

Prince Tyso scrambled to his feet. Tom looked at him through the smoke and then stared down at Aldred's still body.

"I aimed away," Tom began, but smoke from the beams caught in his throat and made him splutter. "I followed my heart and aimed away."

Tyso grabbed his arm. The flames were now out of control and the smoke from the beams was becoming thick and black. It was difficult to see the doorway. Suddenly there was a loud crack from one of the overhead beams. It sagged, groaned and fell crashing to the floor. Tom felt a tug on his arm.

"Quickly." The prince pulled Tom forward.

Another beam fell. The ground was shaking. Tom looked to the doorway. The smoke softened its edges and made it seem further away. Plaster and stone began to rain down and the doorway vanished behind a curtain of rubble. With barely a pause the prince changed direction, pulling Tom now up the steps of the altar to the stained glass window beside it. Tyso drew his sword and launched it at the window, sending the glass spraying out in a multicoloured shower. All that was left of the window was a black gaping hole.

Tom followed the prince onto the ledge of the window. All the benches were burning now, there was nowhere else to go. It was black as pitch outside and looking down from the ledge Tom could not see the ground below him.

"Jump!" cried the prince.

"I can't see what's out there." Tom nervously lifted his foot and shards of glass fell off the sill. There was no sound of them hitting anything below. Inside the Tower, two more beams crashed within moments and Tom thought he felt the sill beneath his feet begin to give. But he had no time to look, because the prince's hand was on his shoulder and the cold wet wind was rushing by him as he plummeted into the darkness below. He might have cried out, or perhaps it was the prince beside him, Tom wasn't sure. He was bracing himself for an almighty crash. He had never broken a limb. He wondered how it would feel. He wished he could faint, but the faint didn't come.

The purple sparks came seconds before he hit the ground. A thunderclap bellowed the moment he landed. The ground was not the solid rock he had been expecting. Everything had changed. Bright light stung his eyes and dry heat took his breath away.

Tom blinked several times and looked around him. To his right the prince was pulling his sword out of the earth and wiping it on the inside of his tunic. He replaced it in the scabbard at his waist. Looking up from the sword

Tom saw two dark blurs in the distance, but it took some time for his eyes to adjust before he realized that the odd shapes were Doug and Silas. Tom had returned to the Whispering Hills, and he had brought the prince with him.

Douglas and Silas sprang to their feet as they spied Tom and the prince approaching out of the heatwaves. As they drew near, Silas bowed to the prince and Douglas repeated the gesture.

"I am at your command," Silas said with an earnest nod.

Unsure of what to say, Douglas nodded too.

The prince offered the boys a smile so sincere and warm that both instantly felt at ease. Douglas suddenly remembered the rider and looked at Tom. "Aldred was here. He had a horse. Did you see him? What happened? You just disappeared."

"He's dead," replied Tom.

"You killed him?"

Slowly, Tom said, "I think he killed himself."

Doug did not look convinced. "You *think*?"

"He fell to the ground." Tom continued. "The Tower is crumbling. He—"

"But how do we know for sure?"

"I... " said Tom, and then he stopped. Something hit his forehead, something soft and warm and wet. A moment later something similar tapped his shoulder with a soft pop. Beside him he heard Silas gasp and then cry, "Look!"

as he jabbed a pointed finger high into the air. Tom thought that Silas looked more frightened now than he ever had in the Forests. "What is it? Is it magic?"

Tom knew. Douglas knew. Prince Tyso, asleep through Edonia's troubled years, recognized it instantly. It was a cloud.

A thick black raincloud painting out the sky like a blot of ink spreading across a clean white sheet.

A drop of water hit Silas and smudged the paste on his face.

Tom couldn't help laughing. "It's rain, Silas. Rain. The droughts are over," he cried with relief. "The curse is lifted."

A moment later a brilliant flash lit up the sky. There was a thunderclap – a real thunderclap – which seemed to shake the ground, and before the rumble faded, the rain became a thick driving downpour.

13

AFTERWORD

To Tom and Douglas, the days that followed were crowded and confusing. As they journeyed to Crestoban the clouds spread and rain followed them. Fresh green shoots, as if waiting for this moment, began to appear in the barren fields.

With the rain spread the news, and ordinary folk – farmers and miners and weavers – joined them on their march on the castle. Two days into the journey, in the market square of a village called Venturii, they met the Resistance – a band of ragged and weary-looking men whose number was small enough to worry Tom. But without Aldred, his Knights of the New Order were confused and demoralized, and the only actual fighting, the battle for possession of the castle at Crestoban, was sharp and swift.

Among the fighters who joined the prince for that final battle was a tall, grey haired man who, because he wore the fine tunic and armour of an Edonian lord, Tom did not at first recognize. It was Lord Nightshade. The old pedlar. Aaron.

Aaron took charge of things after the battle. There was a lot to do. News had to be spread to the Shadow Hills and beyond, and the people banished to the Prairies needed to be returned to look after the tender new seedlings. He sent out riders that very night.

The news spread quickly and when all signs of battle had been removed from the castle, Prince Tyso was crowned King of Edonia in a simple ceremony that also honoured Tom and Douglas and Silas. Time by then was moving on, and the world of the boys and Edonia were drifting apart. That evening, as a rainbow hung over the courtyard, the boys said farewell to their friends.

The new king looked regal, yet his eyes still held their boyish sparkle. There was a new hope in Aaron's face and he no longer appeared old and weary. Silas, with the camouflage paste washed from his face, looked like an ordinary round-faced boy with large brown eyes. Tom thought that Douglas seemed different too. A little older, a little wiser.

Tyso wished them a safe journey and hoped that they would return soon. For all that they had done they were both given, as Silas had, a ring engraved with the royal seal. It would make them welcome anywhere in the land. Perhaps next time their worlds were close, Edonia would be as it used to be.

"Takes care," said Silas.

"Yes," replied Tom. Then he looked at Aaron in his fine new robes, and nodded a final goodbye.

The journey back – through the "Subway" to the field in the Farposts where the burned black oak stood, took them three days. They walked through meadows and slept in clover and kept the delicious snacks, gratefully prepared for them by the castle cooks, to a regular routine. Sooner than expected the oak came into view. Tom stopped before the tree and turned. Way down the field was the old wooden gate which he had used on his first puzzling visit to the Farposts, and for a moment Tom thought he saw the tall grey figure of a gypsy pedlar. A thin twist of smoke was rising from the pipe at his mouth. Then he turned and looked at Douglas and together they walked forward...

The purple sparks washed over them like hot, sparkling rain. When they faded the boys were in Tom's bedroom. It was night-time. October wind rattled the upstairs window-panes and rolled the grass outside in great dark waves toward the distant hills. The clock on Tom's cabinet read eight fifty-four.

Not an hour had passed since they had first plunged through the wall many Edonian days ago.

The house was still. Aunt Jess was out. There was no sign that Aldred had ever been there.

Tom's aunt returned an hour later and asked if they had a good time in the park. It was a shame, she said, that it rained.

"Yes," said Tom, a little too quickly.

Douglas nodded so hard his head swam.

Next day Tom and Douglas visited All Hallows Church, but the church had gone and so had the bulldozers Douglas had earlier mentioned. All that remained was a patch of rubble over which hung a heavy grey raincloud which sent everyone but Tom and Douglas running for cover.

It rained a lot over the next few days, but Tom and Douglas didn't mind. Neither of them ever looked up at a rain-cloud in quite the same way again.